The COLOR
of a
MEMORY

By
Julianne MacLean

ISBN: 1927675197
ISBN 13: 9781927675199

Prologue

Audrey Fitzgerald

I didn't know it at the time, but it was something quite extraordinary that drew my daughter Wendy to the window that morning. In my ignorance, I was simply pleased to have an excuse to leave the dirty dishes behind for later when she said, "Look, Mommy." Her tiny nose was pressed to the glass. "A little girl…"

Wendy was three years old. It was just the two of us then, living alone together in a ground-floor apartment in Manchester, Connecticut. Wendy had very little memory of her father who had died the year before.

He was a firefighter and a great hero on many levels, though I didn't always believe that. We'd had our ups and downs, Alex and I.

But on that particular day, all that mattered to me was my daughter's happiness. As a result, when she asked to go outside and play with the little girl enjoying a picnic with her mother across the street, I was quick to grab our jackets and go.

"Do you live near here?" I asked the girl's mother as we stood in the playground watching our daughters run around in circles.

"We live in Waltham," she replied in a friendly tone of voice. "We're just passing through." Then she noticed her daughter, who looked to be about eighteen months old, struggling to climb up the steps to the big swirly slide. "Pardon me for a second," she said.

She went to help her, and down they went, laughing and squealing.

It was a moment I appreciated because it had been a somber year since my husband's death.

Oh, how I missed that feeling…being able to laugh and experience such joy over simply being alive.

"I confess," I said to the woman when she returned to stand beside me, "that we only came out here because we saw the two of you from our front window. There aren't many kids on this street—at least none Wendy's age. She's an only child."

"My Ellen's an only, too," she told me.

"Are you married?" I asked, not knowing why I suddenly blurted out such a personal question, but I was curious for some reason. There was something familiar about this woman.

She nodded, but didn't meet my gaze. "Just recently, but my husband's working today. You?"

I looked down at my running shoes and wondered when I would be able to answer that question without feeling like I wanted to crawl into bed, curl up in a ball and draw the covers up to my ears.

"I was," I replied, "but my husband passed away about a year ago. He was a firefighter. Died on the job."

The woman said nothing for a moment, then she, too, looked down at the grass and ran the toe of her shoe over a brown patch. "I'm sorry to hear that."

Funny, how the mention of death always casts such a dark shadow over any conversation. I wished I hadn't said anything. I really had to learn to keep my tragic widowhood to myself. Why couldn't I just smile and give the subject of marriage a wide berth?

Later, the woman invited Wendy and me to join her on the blanket for some yogurt and juice. Soon we were chatting about preschools and kid-friendly menu options, and for reasons I didn't understand at the time, she began asking questions about Alex.

Given the circumstances of my relationship with my late husband and how we came to be together, I should have been more suspicious of her—because when it came to Alex and other women, I'd been burned before. Quite literally, in fact.

But this stranger in the park had a way of making me let down my guard. Before I knew it, I was spilling out my whole life story to her—to this person I would later learn was connected to me in the most profound way, in a way I never could have imagined. At least not at the time.

But isn't that what life's all about? Learning new things about ourselves and making sense of our destinies?

How extraordinary it is when all the puzzle pieces finally come together and we are able to see the whole picture...and behold something beautiful.

If someone told me years ago that one day I would become "the other woman," I wouldn't have believed it. I'd been raised by two happily married parents with an iron-clad set of rules about family values.

"You don't cheat," my father said to all of us on a regular basis, pointing his chubby finger at the air. "It's a simple matter of honor."

He and my mother could have been the poster children for every self-help book on the market about how to succeed at marriage. After thirty years, they still held hands and flirted with each other as if they'd just spoken their wedding vows the day before.

I'd always imagined I would end up in a relationship just like theirs—because didn't people say girls usually married carbon copies of their fathers?

I suppose I blew that rule out of the water on the day I met Alex Fitzgerald for the first time—because he was exactly the sort of man my father always warned me *against*.

Too handsome for his own good. And Lord, did he know it.

66 "A re you Alex Fitzgerald?" I asked as I pulled back the blue curtain in the ER and regarded the dark-haired firefighter on the bed. He wore a black T-shirt and faded blue jeans, and smirked at me like he was Colin Farrell.

"Yep."

Standing with my pen hovering over the chart on my clipboard, I said, "Can you tell me what happened?"

There was a second firefighter in the room as well. He stood beside the bed. Tall and broad-shouldered, he was equally handsome but with honey-colored hair. He bowed his head and chuckled.

Alex gave him a smack with the back of his hand before he answered my question. "Don't make fun, David, or my pretty nurse will ask you to leave."

My eyes lifted and I regarded them both without humor.

"He dropped a fire extinguisher on his foot," David explained.

My next enquiry was directed at the patient. "What part of your foot, exactly?"

David chuckled again.

"What did I just tell ya?" Alex said to his friend with a laugh. Then he swept me a flirtatious glance with those dark-lashed brown eyes, and smiled. "Though maybe it would be *better* if he left. Is he distracting you, Nurse…?" He sat forward to squint at my badge. "Nurse Audrey. That's a very pretty name."

I lowered the clipboard to my side and glanced from one firefighter to the other. They each wore tight T-shirts that shamelessly flaunted their muscular upper bodies. The testosterone in the room was palpable, but I'd had a rough morning with a difficult pediatric case—possible leukemia—that left me in no mood for barroom pickup lines.

"Any smoke inhalation?" I asked, pushing my glasses up the bridge of my nose.

David, the blonde one, was quick to pipe in and answer the question. "No, you've got it all wrong. Alex was stuffing his face with French fries at the station and his hands were all greasy. He picked up an empty extinguisher to move it off a chair so he could sit down and take a load off, but it slipped through his fingers. Ketchup flew everywhere, and it was quite the ordeal. He thinks something's broken."

I inclined my head at Alex, who didn't appear to be in much pain at all. "Is that what happened?"

"It's dangerous work sometimes," he replied.

I glanced down at Alex's sneaker. "Well, hotshot. You're going to have to remove that shoe so the doctor can examine you. The sock, too."

Without warning, one of the other nurses whipped the privacy curtain back and I jumped. "Can you come over to bed six?" she asked. "I need help with an IV."

"I'll be right there," I smoothly replied. Then I met my patient's gaze. "I'll be back in two minutes."

"I'll be waiting," he replied with a playful note of seduction in his voice that made me shake my head in disbelief as I turned away.

When I pulled back the curtain on Mr. Hotshot Firefighter a few minutes later, he was sitting up on the edge of the bed.

Shirtless.

Though I was a practical and levelheaded woman by nature, I couldn't ignore the fact that I was standing before a ridiculously extravagant plethora of bronzed, rippling muscles that must have taken years of workouts at the gym to achieve. I couldn't help but laugh at the proud spectacle before me. This man was unbelievable. "I said the shoe, not the shirt."

"No, I'm sure you said the shirt," he innocently replied. "Don't you have to listen to my heart or something? Take my blood pressure...I did feel a bit woozy when it happened."

It had been an utterly wretched day for the most part, so I decided at last to surrender to the comedy of this moment. Striding forward, I removed my stethoscope from the pocket of my uniform and kept my eyes fixed on his as I touched the scope to his chest. "Where did your friend go?"

"I told him I didn't need a babysitter," Alex replied. "He's probably chatting up some young nursing student by now."

I nodded my head. "I see. You two are quite the pair. I can't imagine what sort of trouble you must get into on a Saturday night."

"Oh, no," Alex replied. "We're not like that."

I chuckled. "Says the man who couldn't wait to strip off his T-shirt for the poor unsuspecting nurse."

He slanted me a look. "Poor, unsuspecting? Pardon me for sayin' so, Nurse Audrey, but those aren't the words I would use to describe *you*."

With no intention of falling for his charms, I gave no reply and focused on the task of taking his blood pressure.

"I guess I don't need to ask you to roll up your sleeve… since you aren't wearing one," I mentioned with dry sarcasm as I wrapped the cuff around his generous bicep.

"Do you have a boyfriend, Nurse Audrey?" Alex asked as I pumped air into the BP cuff.

Timing the pulse in the crook of his arm, I chose to ignore the question. Then I tugged at the Velcro and removed the cuff. "Blood pressure looks good," I said. "You're healthy as a horse."

The resident doctor walked in. "Hey there," he casually said, sliding his hands into the pockets of his lab coat. "What's up?"

"This is Alex Fitzgerald," I explained. "He's a firefighter and he dropped an extinguisher on his foot. He thinks it might be broken."

"Sounds like you had an off day." Dr. Grant moved around the foot of the bed and patted the mattress. "How about swinging your legs right up here."

Backing out of the way, I watched while Dr. Grant examined Alex's foot. He pressed the pads of his thumbs in different areas and asked all sorts of questions.

He made no comment about the fact that Alex was shirtless.

"It does look like something might be broken," Dr. Grant said to me. "We're going to need an X-ray to see what we're dealing with, so take him up to radiology and let me know as soon as you have the results."

"Sure," I replied.

After he left, Alex inclined his head at me and spoke cheerfully. "Looks like we'll get to spend some more time together, Nurse Audrey."

"Not until you put your shirt back on," I replied matter-of-factly as I went to fetch a wheelchair.

⸻

Over the next five hours, I kept abreast of Alex's case. The X-ray images revealed that he had broken two of his metatarsals, which are good-sized bones in his foot. This surprised me because most people are pasty gray and do a fair bit of moaning and complaining when they arrive in the ER with even the smallest fracture.

But Alex was a trooper and managed to get through all the poking and prodding with a sense of humor, pouring on the charm to all the nurses, even the older ones. Especially them. After a while I began to relax and stopped assuming he was just trying to pick me up. In fact, it lifted my spirits to see the older ladies blush.

When at last he was discharged with a cast boot on his foot, I was just finishing my shift, so I volunteered to push him in the wheelchair onto the elevator to take him down to the front lobby.

"You never answered my question," he said when the elevator doors closed and we were alone.

"What question was that?"

"I asked if you had a boyfriend," he reminded me.

For a long moment I stared at the floor indicator above the doors and watched the numbers count down. When the display flashed L and I knew it was time to get off, I said with a sigh of defeat, "No, I don't have a boyfriend."

The doors opened. I pushed the chair forward.

As we were rolling out, he tipped his head all the way back to look up at me, and I found myself smiling down at his face, which was no less handsome from that angle.

"You're a good nurse," he said. "I'm glad it was you today."

"I'll bet you say that to all the girls," I replied with a smile.

"Nope, just you. So how about you let me buy you dinner?"

"I don't think so."

"At least tell me your last name. Or give me your phone number."

I grinned down at him. "Not a chance." Then I briefly glanced up to make sure I wasn't about to steer him down a steep flight of stairs. That wouldn't be good.

He faced forward as well. "Then don't be surprised if you see me again next week with some other random ailment. Maybe I'll develop a pain in my side that will take hours to diagnose."

"Didn't you ever hear the story about the boy who cried wolf?" I asked. "That didn't end well."

He tilted his head back again. "Then maybe you should just give me your number."

I laughed and shook my head at him then realized we were about to collide with a woman who was standing directly in our path to the door.

I pulled the chair to a halt and Alex jolted forward.

"Melanie," he said, seeming startled to see her.

"Hey." She glanced at me suspiciously, then adjusted her purse strap on her shoulder. "Who's this?"

"This is Audrey," Alex replied. "She's my nurse. Audrey, this is Melanie."

"Hi," I casually said, waving a hand.

Melanie was tall and supermodel-skinny with blonde hair, full lips and big eyes—eyes that glared at me with venom.

"I thought David was picking me up," Alex said to her.

"I told him I'd do it," she replied. "Why didn't you call me earlier? I would have come right away. Is it broken?"

He lifted the cast boot to show her. "Yeah. Guess I'll be off work for a few weeks."

"Bummer," Melanie said. "Are you ready to go? I can bring the car around."

"That would be great. Thanks."

Melanie hurried off, leaving Alex and me alone to wait inside. I set the brake on the chair and sat down on the window ledge to face him.

"Who's Melanie?" I asked point blank. "Your sister? Cousin? Housekeeper, maybe?"

His eyes were fixed on the view of the parking lot outside the glass. "She's not my girlfriend," he said. "Well, she sort of is. She *was*."

I held up a hand. "Don't bother to explain. It's none of my business."

We waited in silence for a moment.

"So I guess dinner Friday night is out of the question?" he asked, turning his head to look at me.

"Yep. Totally out of the question."

His chest rose and fell with a heavy sigh, and he nodded his head, as if he wasn't surprised.

Melanie came speeding up to the entrance in a sporty little lime-green Volkswagen convertible. She pulled to a halt and got out to open the passenger side door.

I rolled Alex outside, set the brake again, and he hobbled out of the chair and into the front seat.

"Thanks, Audrey," he said as I backed up and rolled the chair out of the way.

"No problem. Take care, now."

He shut the car door and Melanie hit the gas. They sped off into the hazy evening sunset. For a moment I stood alone, watching the car grow distant, then I returned inside to grab my stuff and go home.

⌒

Over the next few days, I thought about Alex Fitzgerald more often than I cared to admit and it bothered me how much he was on my mind. I hardly knew the guy, and he certainly wasn't my type because he was too much of a flirt. I had seen dozens of patients that day. Why should I be thinking of *him*?

Because he looked great shirtless?

Needless to say, I made sure I worked hard to purge him from my mind, but I also felt sorry for Melanie who was clearly devoted to him while he was asking other women out on dates.

I decided I wouldn't want to be in her shoes. Not in a million years.

Looking back on it, I wish I had mentioned the encounter to someone, because that's when the phone calls began. It would have been helpful to have had a record of everything.

Three

The first call occurred when I arrived home from the movies on a Saturday night. The call display said "Private Caller," so I picked it up. "Hello?"

My greeting was met with a few seconds of silence, which made me think it was a telemarketer. I was about to press the end call button, but the unknown caller hung up before I had a chance to.

It happened again the following morning at eight o'clock, waking me from a very deep sleep. I flopped across the bed and answered groggily, "Hello?"

Again I was met with silence on the other end, then *click*. The line went dead.

"Thanks a lot," I replied as I ended the call and tried, unsuccessfully, to go back to sleep.

How foolish I was to think it was a wrong number, but my night shift hours that week had left me in a daze.

But eventually, I *would* wake from it.

I didn't work another shift until Tuesday night, which gave me time to attend a spinning class that morning and meet my friend Cathy for lunch downtown.

Cathy and I had known each other since high school and I was her maid of honor the previous summer when she married Bob, the guy she met in college.

Bob was an electrician but he was working with some filmmaker pals on a reality TV show about rewiring old houses. Bob was smart and funny and we all knew he'd make a terrific host. They just had to pitch their idea to a network willing to take a chance on the idea.

As for Cathy, she was the most generous, easygoing person I knew, and she worked part-time for an insurance company.

"Audrey, why don't we go down to the fire station after lunch and ask how that hot firefighter's doing?" she suggested when our soups and salads arrived. "I'm sure someone will know. Didn't you say he brought a friend to the ER? We could ask that guy."

"I'm not going down there," I replied, "because I have no desire to find out how he's doing. And why do you keep bringing it up?"

"Because you told me what he looked like shirtless and what a jerk he was for cheating on his girlfriend. You *never* talk about patients like that. Isn't there some rule about confidentiality?"

"I also never went out with him," I replied, "so in actuality, he didn't cheat on his girlfriend. And confidentiality hasn't been breached because I didn't tell you his name."

She wagged her salad fork at me. "But he would have cheated on her if you had said yes to the date."

I shook my head. "I still don't even know if she *was* his girlfriend. He was pretty vague about it."

"There, you see?" Cathy said. "You're still curious about him."

I looked down at my minestrone soup. "No, I'm not."

"You're the biggest liar I know."

"Maybe so," I replied with a chuckle, "but I'm still not going down to the fire station."

—⸺

I had been manning the nurse's station for a few hours that night when Jason, the clerk beside me, tapped me on the shoulder. "Audrey?"

I looked up from the computer screen to find myself staring blankly at Alex Fitzgerald. He stood on crutches on the other side of the desk.

"Hey," I said, blinking my eyes to try and gain some focus. "What are you doing here? Is everything okay?"

As if he were pulling a rabbit out of a hat, he whipped out a big bunch of colorful spring flowers and held them out. "These are for you."

Leaning back in my chair, folding my arms across my chest, I laughed. "What for?"

"To say thank you."

I regarded him skeptically. "I was just doing my job."

"But you did it brilliantly." He glanced at Jason who was standing beside me, listening to our conversation with interest. "I'm here to ask her out for dinner, but I'm afraid she's going to say no."

Jason nudged me with his elbow. *Hard.* "Come on, Audrey. Throw the guy a bone. He came all the way down here on crutches. The least you could do is have something to eat with him."

"I'm working," I reminded them both.

"You have a supper break coming up," Jason was happy to add. "She usually eats in the cafeteria," he told Alex.

Alex held out the flowers again. "Perfect. I love cafeteria food, and these need to be put in water."

Jason reached across the desk to take them. "I'll handle that."

"You're not helping," I called out to Jason over my shoulder as he went off in search of a suitable container.

Alex smiled at me.

"How's your foot?" I asked him.

"Better," he replied. "I'm getting around okay. How's everything with you?"

"Fine and dandy."

We regarded each other for a long, intense moment, then I laughed softly in defeat.

"So is that a yes?" Alex asked, tilting his head to the side.

Jason returned with the flowers, set them down on the desk in front of me and nudged me again with his elbow.

I let out a breathless sigh. "I guess so. As long as you promise to keep your shirt on this time."

Alex held up a few fingers. "Scout's honor. At least for today."

I tossed my pencil onto the desk and went to grab my purse, feeling quite certain that agreeing to have dinner with Alex Fitzgerald was going to be one of the worst mistakes of my life.

"Just so you know," I said as we stepped onto the elevator. "I don't date guys who have girlfriends." I pushed the button for the cafeteria floor.

"Perfect," he said. "Neither do I."

A few other people got on behind us and the doors closed. Neither of us spoke until the doors opened again and we got off.

"And she's not my girlfriend," Alex said, falling into pace beside me on his crutches.

"But she used to be," I said—just to make sure I had all the facts straight.

Alex nodded. "Yes."

I considered that for a moment. "Does she know she's not your girlfriend anymore? Because she didn't seem too pleased to see you flirting with me the other day."

"If anyone was flirting, it was *you*," he teasingly replied.

I couldn't help but laugh softly as we entered the cafeteria and I grabbed two trays, one for each of us.

"See, you're still doing it," he said.

I laughed again. "And who came down here with the flowers?"

He smiled at me. "Fine. You win."

We ordered our meals and I carried both our trays, one at a time, to a table.

"Maybe I should have waited until I got the cast off to ask you out," he said as he sat down across from me. "I don't think I'm making the right impression."

"And what impression would that be?"

"That I'm a stand-up guy. Reliable. Dependable."

"It takes more than two good feet to be dependable," I told him. "So where's Melanie tonight?"

"I don't know. I told you, she's not my girlfriend anymore."

Looking down at my pasta, I rummaged around for the onions and picked them out with my fork. "I hope you didn't break her heart just for me—because I'm a busy person. I'm not looking for anything."

"It's been over between Melanie and me for a while."

My eyes lifted. "Does *she* know that?"

"Of course. We're just friends now."

I finished picking out the onions. "So how long were you together? If you don't mind my asking...?"

He shrugged a shoulder. "It wasn't that serious. We met in a bar and dated for about six months. What can I say? She's a gorgeous girl—"

I picked up the roll on my plate and spread butter on it. "I noticed."

"But enough about my love life," Alex said, reaching for his water. "Tell me about you. What made you decide to go into nursing?"

I finished chewing, then decided to let go of the subject of past girlfriends. I told him bits and pieces about my life and career choices.

Then I asked what made him decide to go into firefighting, and before I knew it, we were swapping war stories about our jobs, and my supper break was over.

He reached for his crutches and I carried both trays to the trolley.

Maybe it was a mistake, but this time, when we walked out together and he asked for my number...I gave it to him.

~⏤⏳

Later that night when I arrived home after my shift, I made the foolish assumption that raccoons had gotten into my garbage.

With everything strewn all over my lawn at the curb, there was no way I could wait until the morning to clean it up. It was already past midnight and the garbage truck would come by at 7:00 a.m. So I went inside to fetch a pair of rubber gloves and tackled the grubby task of bagging everything up again.

Afterward, I took a quick shower before I fell, oblivious, into bed.

CHAPTER

Five

⌒⌒⌒

I woke late the next morning, made a pot of coffee, then stepped outside in my bathrobe and slippers to fetch up the newspaper. As I unrolled it in the bright sunshine, I noticed that the garbage man had collected my trash and left the plastic bins empty on their sides at the curb. There were only a few indiscriminate traces of the raccoon invasion—some small wrappers and tissues in the grass—things I'd missed in the dark which I resolved to pick up later, after I got dressed.

Returning to the kitchen, I cooked myself some scrambled eggs, sat down at the table and read the paper while I ate.

Later, while I was loading my dirty dishes into the dishwasher, the telephone rang.

It said "Private Caller."

I stared at it for a moment.

Tapping my fingers on the countertop, I grew increasingly irritated as I debated whether or not to answer.

In the end, I picked it up after the fourth ring. "Hello?"

There was no response, but I could hear something in the background. It sounded like a blender running.

"Hello!" I shouted into the phone. Then *click*, they hung up.

Letting out an angry huff, I scrolled through the previous calls and noted with some unease that there had been five missed calls the night before while I was at work, all from "Private Caller."

Frowning, I speed-dialed Cathy. "Hey, you haven't been phoning me from some other number have you?"

"No," she replied. "Why?"

I bent to grab the box of dishwasher detergent under the sink and poured powder into the dispenser. "Because someone keeps calling me and hanging up. They called five times last night while I was at work." I shut the dishwasher door and pressed the start button.

"Probably those stupid telemarketers," Cathy said. "Did you check the Caller ID?"

"Yeah, it says Private Caller."

"Well, that sucks. You know there's a website where you can get your number removed from lists. I forget what it's called but I'll get Bob to email you the link."

"Thanks. Can you make it to spinning class today?"

"Not today," she replied. "I'm swamped here. Maybe tomorrow though."

"Okay." We made quick plans for the following morning and hung up.

I went into the bedroom to get dressed, then outside to drag the empty trash containers back from the curb and pick up the last remnants of rubbish in the grass.

When I returned to the kitchen, the phone was ringing again, but this time, there was someone on the other end of the line. My heart began to race.

It was Alex who called, and I was embarrassed to admit how giddy I became just from the sound of his voice in my ear. Though I knew he was a shameless flirt—and I certainly didn't trust him to be the sort of man I always imagined myself ending up with—I couldn't resist him. I was flattered by his attention and becoming increasingly infatuated by the minute. He was just so darn attractive. The physical attraction knocked me completely off balance.

At first he apologized for his physical incapacity and explained that under normal circumstances he would be a far more exciting cohort. He assured me he would be taking me to the beach, or bungee jumping, or dancing in a club. As it stood, he couldn't even drive his car, so picking me up for dinner was out of the question as well.

"How did you get to the hospital last night?" I asked. "Did you take a bus?"

"David gave me a lift," he replied, "and he picked me up afterward."

"That was good of him," I said.

"He's the best."

Alex then invited me over to his place for lunch, and I could do nothing but say, "Hell, yes."

When I pulled up in front of Alex's house at noon, I was surprised by the look of the place. It was a white stucco century home with a rock garden and mature trees in the yard, situated in an established upscale neighborhood.

I didn't know what kind of salary firefighters earned, but I was quite certain that a young, single guy like Alex couldn't possibly afford a property like this. Unless he came from money. Or had recently become divorced from an heiress.

Gathering my purse and keys, I stepped out of my car—a beat up old '76 Mustang I bought a few years back—and crossed the driveway to ring the bell. It took a few moments for Alex to answer, and when he opened the door, the first thing he did was apologize.

"Sorry to keep you waiting. I can't move very fast." He stepped back to invite me in.

"Where are your crutches?" I asked.

"I get tired of picking them up and setting them down," he explained, returning to the kitchen. "You'll have to start calling me Hop-along."

I laughed and glanced around at the classic décor inside. The woodwork in the home boasted elegant turn-of-the-century character, but the furniture was sleek and modern. "What a beautiful home."

"Thanks," he said, "but it's not my house. It's my parents'. I've been staying here for the past few days because my apartment is up two flights of stairs. No elevator."

"I see." That explained things.

"My mother's been spoiling me," he added as he gestured for me to follow him into the kitchen, which had obviously been remodeled recently with white cupboards, granite countertops and stainless steel appliances.

"Are your parents here?" I asked.

"No, Mom and my stepdad are at work. I'm going out of my mind sitting around here all by myself. I'm glad you could come over."

I shrugged. "Guess those are the perks of working the night shift." I set my purse down on one of the chocolate-brown leather stools at the island bar. "And thanks for inviting me. It smells good…whatever you're cooking."

"It's just spaghetti," he said. "I'm not much of a gourmet."

"Can I do anything to help?"

He pointed to the bowl of salad on the counter. "You could take that outside to the back deck and grab a bottle of wine from the rack on the island. The corkscrew's in the drawer below."

I moved to the floor-to-ceiling French windows and peered out at a teakwood table on a small, private flagstone patio. It was nestled cozily among lush and leafy elderberry hedges. Wild flowers bloomed everywhere, and colorful bird feeders and hanging glass ornaments made the space look like a magical fairyland.

Grabbing the salad bowl in one hand, I pulled a bottle of wine out of the rack on the counter and carried everything out. When I returned for glasses, utensils and the cork screw, Alex was lifting the large pot of boiling noodles to the sink to pour into the strainer, managing quite impressively to hobble on one foot.

"You sure you don't need any help?" I asked.

"I got this," he replied.

He served up two plates of linguine with a thick and meaty sauce that made my mouth water. Then he smothered them in fresh parmesan.

"At least let me carry the plates out," I said with a smile.

A few minutes later we were seated in the sunshine, sipping red wine and enjoying the meal.

"What time did you get home last night?" he asked.

"It was crazy in the ER," I explained. "I had to stay late to finish out a case, so it was nearly midnight. Then I came home to find my garbage strewn all over my lawn. Stupid raccoons must have gotten into it. I wasn't happy about that."

He twirled his linguine around his fork. "What kind of bins do you have?"

"The cheap kind," I replied. "The lids never stay on."

"Remind me, before you go, to show you the ones my parents use. They're around the side of the garage. Nothing can get into those suckers. They're like army tanks."

"I'd love to see them." I sat back in my chair and laughed. "This is quite the conversation for a second date."

He grinned at me. "Am I impressing you yet? Living with my parents…. Hopping on one foot…. Bragging about trash cans."

"You're different, I'll give you that."

We chatted about his parents' house for a while, but he told me this wasn't where he grew up. Before his father died they had lived in a different neighborhood.

"When did he pass away?" I asked.

"He died of cancer when I was nine," Alex explained. "My mom raised my sister and me on her own after that. It took her a long time to get over losing him. She finally remarried six years ago and moved in here with Garry."

"What does Garry do?" I asked.

"He owns Chesterton Construction."

I gulped down a mouthful of spaghetti. "Wow."

No wonder they could afford to live in this neighborhood. Chesterton Construction built office towers and condos, and developed sprawling subdivisions on the outskirts of the city.

"So what do you think of Garry?" I asked. "Is he a good match for your mom?"

"He's great," Alex said. "I'm glad she finally found someone, especially now that Sarah and I are grown up and moved out."

"Sarah's your sister?"

He nodded and picked up his wine. "Yeah, younger sister. She's going to university in Boston. She's a handful, that one."

"How so?"

He set down his glass. "She was always getting into trouble in high school. Hanging out with the wrong crowd. Playing hooky."

"But she's in university now, so that's promising."

"Yeah, but she's in a sorority," he said, "having the time of her life. I just hope she doesn't flunk out."

"How's your mom handling that?"

"It's always been rough, but she never loses faith. She believes in Sarah, trusts that she's smart and she'll figure everything out eventually."

I sat back in my chair and breathed in the refreshing floral scents of the patio. "It must be hard being a parent, watching your kids make mistakes." A hummingbird hovered at the feeder behind Alex's head. I stared at it for a moment until it flew away. "I think the best parents don't try to protect their kids too much. They let them go out into the world and learn for themselves."

Alex nodded. "I agree. What about your parents? Where are they?"

I was feeling the wine now, and the warmth of the sun on my cheeks made me want to recline in a lounge chair somewhere and contemplate the universe. "They live in Stamford. My dad manages a hardware store and my mom's a teacher."

"Do you see them much?"

"Not as much as I should," I replied. "It's tough when I work so many weird hours. I'm always catching up on sleep."

"I know what you mean," he said. "I work odd hours, too."

"That's what we get for choosing careers in emergency services," I replied.

"Yep. Serves us right, but I wouldn't trade it for the world."

"Me neither."

We gazed at each other across the table for a moment.

Suddenly I worried that I had become *too* relaxed. As I was driving over here, I'd promised myself I would keep up my guard, not let him mesmerize me with his good looks and amusing conversation.

But I liked him. I enjoyed talking with him and I wanted to know more about his life and his family and all the things that were important to him. There was an obvious connection between us and I wondered if he was simply one of those people who made everyone feel comfortable.

"So are you going to show me those trash cans or what?" I asked when we finished eating.

"Sure." He pushed his chair back to rise. "And there's something else I want to show you, too. Let's clear the table first."

"Good idea. Can't take any chances with those crazy Manchester raccoons."

As I followed him to the kitchen, I wondered what it was he wanted to show me.

CHAPTER

Seven

⌒⌒⌒

"Wow," I said as I ran my hand over the shiny black hood of the vintage car in the garage. "What year is it?"

"It's a 1948 Buick Street Rod. I thought you might like to see it because I noticed you pulled up in a '76 Mustang. Is that yours?"

"Yeah, I bought it a few years ago." I bent to peer in the side window of the Buick. "It needs work but I don't know anything about restoring old cars. I just liked it and it was cheap."

"You should let me take a look at it," Alex said as he watched me move around the old car. "I've been working on this baby for a while and there's not much else to do with her. I just come out here every once in a while…dust her off…polish her fender. Since I'm going to be off work for the next few weeks, I could use a new project."

I straightened and regarded him over the hood. "Yeah?"

He nodded.

"Only if you let me help you," I said. "I'm interested. I'd like to learn."

"Sure."

I felt a sudden rush of excitement. Returning my attention to the Buick, I ran a finger along the shiny door handle. "Can I get in?" I asked.

"Go ahead. It's open."

Simultaneously, we opened both doors. Alex got into the driver's seat and I got in beside him. We shut the doors and sat there. I checked out the vintage dash and looked up at the ceiling.

"How long have you had it?" I asked.

"Forever. It belonged to my dad. It was his first car. He bought it when he was seventeen and never parted with it. It's my favorite memory of being with him as a kid. I remember how he used to take me and my sister to the race track on Saturdays. He'd bet on the horses while Sarah and I would run off to a creek on the far side of the track behind the stables. We used to catch frogs and tadpoles. When he died, Mom put the car in storage and I didn't see it for nearly two decades. A few years ago, I finally went down to the facility and got it out, started to put some work into it. Garry was helpful. He taught me a lot. You should have seen it before."

"You did a great job. I wonder what it's worth now. Probably a lot."

"I have no idea," Alex said, "but it doesn't really matter because I'll never sell it. Someday I'll give it to my son."

I narrowed my eyes at him. "What if you have a daughter?"

He thought about that for a moment. "Then I suppose she'll be the one to get the keys on her sixteenth birthday."

I laughed. "You'd trust a sixteen-year-old to drive this priceless heirloom?"

He considered that as well. "You're right. What am I thinking? Maybe I should just get a giant glass case to store it in."

We sat for a moment in silence, contemplating things.

"Do you ever take it out on the road?" I asked.

"I have, but not often," he replied, palming the wheel. "I'll tell you what—when I get this cast off, I'll take you out cruising on a Friday night. We'll go for ice cream."

"I'd love that."

As I leaned my head back on the seat and smiled across at him, I was struck by a clear and vivid image of my future—but it wasn't what you're thinking.

The premonition caught me off guard and I was confused by it. I won't tell you what it was. Not yet, because I don't want you to feel as if this story is flying off the rails.

Alex and I began to see each other regularly after our lunch date at his parents' house, where we sat for over two hours in the front seat of the Buick, talking about life, work, movies…you name it.

I met his mother when she came home at five o'clock. Her name was Jean and she was a lovely woman with an infectious laugh. She asked me to come for a barbeque that weekend, and I graciously accepted her invitation.

Because I was working a lot of evening shifts that week, I was able to visit Alex in the afternoons. That's when we began working on my Mustang. He ordered some replacement parts for it online and took care of some rust spots for me.

Through our mutual interest in restoring the car, we began to explore the vintage car community online. There were all sorts of clubs and rallies and chat rooms where we found answers to many of our questions and curiosities.

The attraction between us continued to grow, and by the end of the week, I surrendered to his overtures. Before I knew it, we were making out like a couple of teenagers in the back seat of his Buick. When we heard his mother pull into the driveway that day, we had to scramble out of there in a hurry. It was the most fun I'd had since…

Well, I couldn't remember when.

⟲

Thankfully, I received no more phone calls from the mysterious "Private Caller," but something else happened when I returned home from the barbeque at Alex's parents' house on Saturday night.

I unlocked my front door, entered and dropped my purse and keys on the chair. It was nearly one o'clock in the morning but I was wide awake because of my work schedule, so I turned on the TV, then kicked off my flip flops and went to get a glass of water.

As I was filling my glass at the sink, something drew my gaze to the back door. The window beside it was open.

A fireball of panic exploded in my belly—because I was certain I hadn't opened it that day.

Swallowing uneasily, I shut off the water and set my glass down on the counter. My gaze darted to the knife block. I moved toward it and pulled out the eight-inch chef's blade with the pointy tip.

Holding it at my side, I strained to detect any noise in the house. All I heard were the actors' voices on *Law and Order*, and I wished I'd turned on *The Simpsons* instead.

My pulse raced as I crossed the kitchen to the back hall and moved quietly to check both bedrooms. I searched my own room first—looked under the bed and inside the closet—then I checked the guest bedroom which doubled as a place to store all my junk. The closet was clear and there was no one hiding behind the shower curtain in the bathroom either.

Nevertheless, my heart was still pounding like a drum, and I held the knife in a deathlike grip at eye-level as I moved through the house.

Oh, God. I had to check the basement next.

I really didn't want to go down there and thought about calling the police instead. But honestly…by then I wasn't sure… Maybe I *did* open the window that day. I might have done it without thinking because I'd been distracted lately, thinking about Alex.

Oh, screw it. I grabbed my cell phone and dialed his number.

"Hi, sorry to call so late."

"No problem," he said. "What's up?"

In my panic, I was breathing heavily. "I know this sounds crazy, but I came home to find the kitchen window wide open, and I'm totally freaked out. I didn't think I left it like that when I came over to your place, but I might have. I just checked the house and there's no one here and nothing seems to be missing, but I feel like I should check the basement, and it's dark and scary down there."

"Shit," he said. "If I didn't have this cast on, I'd come right over. Want me to call David? He's at the station tonight which isn't far from your place. He could be there in five minutes."

"Yes, please," I said. "Will he mind?"

"No, he'll love it," Alex replied. "Don't hang up. I'll call him from the land line."

"Okay." I didn't like being in the house alone when someone might be hiding in my basement, so I hurried to the front door to wait outside on the step.

I listened to Alex call David and was relieved when he told me David was on his way.

"Thanks so much for coming," I said, rising from the deck chair on my front step. "I'm really sorry Alex had to call you. I feel like an idiot."

"It's no problem," David replied, stepping out of his Jetta and quietly pushing the car door closed. "It was time for my break anyway."

I held my cell phone up to my ear again. "Alex? David's here now. I'll call you back later."

"No, I'll stay on the line," he replied, "just in case David gets jumped."

"You're joking, right?" I asked.

"Of course," he replied, but I sensed that he wasn't.

I hadn't seen or spoken to David since that first day when he brought Alex to the ER, so it felt strange to have him here after dark on a Saturday night, taking care of this for me.

I opened the door and followed him inside. "The basement is this way." I led him to the door, opened it and flicked on the lights.

We both peered down the steps. "Basements are creepy on the best of days," he whispered. "Do you have a baseball bat or something?"

"Um…" I glanced around. "How about a frying pan?"

"That'll do."

I tiptoed to the dish rack, picked up my square-shaped, cast-iron skillet with grill ribs and handed it to him.

"I just gave David a frying pan to use as a weapon," I whispered into the phone, wanting to give Alex a play-by-play report.

"Don't tell him that," David whispered to me. "I'll never hear the end of it."

He started down the steps. "Should I come with you?" I asked.

"No. Stay here and call 911 if I start screaming."

"Did you hear that?" I whispered into the phone.

"I heard it," Alex replied.

David reached the bottom of the stairs and disappeared from view. My heart raced the entire time while I listened to the sound of him moving around down there, no doubt checking every nook and cranny.

A moment later he came up the steps with the frying pan at his side. "All clear, but I think you might have a mouse problem. I saw some droppings behind the furnace."

"Really?" My shoulders relaxed at the news that there was no intruder, but I wasn't thrilled to learn there were rodents scurrying around in my basement.

"Do you have any traps?" he asked.

"Yeah, I think so." I pulled open the junk drawer in my kitchen and dug around at the back. "Here...found some. These are old, but they should still work."

I handed them to David and he pulled them out of the plastic wrapper.

"These are good. Got any cheese?" I fetched some out of the fridge, cut a few small pieces and handed them to him. "I'll be right back," he said, disappearing down the basement stairs again.

Suddenly I realized I'd left Alex waiting on the phone. "Are you still there?" I asked him.

"Yeah, I'm here."

"He found mouse droppings."

"Better than Freddy Krueger," he replied.

I laughed. "Don't say that. Now I'm not going to be able to sleep tonight."

"You can always come over here if you'd be more comfortable," he said.

"To your parents' house? That would be kind of weird, wouldn't it?"

"No. You could sleep in the guest room."

I listened to David poking around in the basement, setting the traps. Then he came back up.

"That's tempting," I said to Alex, "but I'll be fine. I'll make sure all the doors and windows are locked when David leaves. Thanks for your help. I don't know what I would have done without you."

"No problem," Alex replied. "I'll see you tomorrow."

David flicked off the lights in the basement. "All clear," he said, "but you should check those traps once a day to see if you catch anything."

"I will. But listen…Before you go, would you mind checking the bedrooms for me? I'll rest easier if you do."

"Sure."

David made a full sweep of the house and found nothing, then he took a flashlight out to the backyard and searched everywhere, behind the shrubs in the garden and under the deck.

Afterward I walked him to the door and thanked him again.

"Anytime," he said.

I watched him back out of the driveway, then hunkered down on the sofa to watch TV.

⟶ᴄ

At 5:00 a.m., I woke up and glanced at the clock on my bedside table. Feeling groggy and ill at ease—enough to make my stomach churn— I slipped out of bed and padded down the hall to the bathroom.

I flicked on the light, approached the mirror and frowned at my reflection beneath the eerie fluorescent glow. My eyes grew wide and I sucked in a breath of ice-cold terror, because there were handprints around my neck...

Gasping for air, I sat bolt upright on the sofa. All the lights were on in the living room, and an infomercial was playing on TV.

I touched a hand to my throat. "It was just a dream."

Then I reached for my phone to check the time. It was only 4:00 a.m. Still dark out.

Lying back on the sofa, I closed my eyes and cupped my forehead in a hand.

Living alone had never bothered me before. In fact, I'd always felt rather proud of myself for becoming a homeowner at the age of twenty-five, but this was ridiculous.

I wondered if I should get a dog.

Or maybe a roommate was what I needed—but with my luck, I'd end up with Jennifer Jason Leigh from *Single White Female.*

I rolled over to face the TV and hoped everything would feel less sinister in the morning.

Two days later, Alex moved back into his own apartment—a slightly rundown, third-floor flat not far from the fire station. He said he was tired of living out of his suitcase at his parents' house and wanted to be among his own things. I suspected, however, that what he really wanted was privacy, so that we wouldn't have to make out in the back seat of his old Buick anymore.

With this I was completely on board, because let's face it—he was the most attractive man I'd ever dated. I was falling so hard and fast, I felt like I should strap on a parachute.

Alex and I continued to see each other in the afternoons. Usually I picked him up at his apartment and brought him to my house so we could work on my Mustang. We also went out for lunch a few times and took in a matinee.

The following week, however, my work schedule switched back to days, and that's when my world began to spin in unexpected circles.

It was raining buckets when I finished a day shift and walked out of the hospital. I didn't have an umbrella, so I pulled my coat over my head and dashed across the parking lot to my car.

Alex and I had made plans for dinner and I was supposed to pick him up at 6:00, but I suspected he was bored to tears stuck in his apartment all day, so I decided to surprise him and go straight there from the hospital.

Traffic was slow because of the rain and my windshield wiper was acting up again, leaving wide smears of water directly in my line of vision. I considered pulling over and flicking the blade, but didn't want to get soaked, so I continued on.

Turning onto Alex's street, I slowed down to look for a parking spot along the curb, but my stomach dropped when I saw, parked out front, a familiar little lime-green convertible.

What the hell was Melanie doing there at three-thirty in the afternoon? Alex had assured me more than once that it was over between them.

There were no empty parking spaces on the street, and even if there were, I wouldn't have taken it—because the last thing I wanted to do was knock on Alex's door and find a beautiful supermodel lounging on his sofa.

As I drove away, the rain pounded harder against my windshield.

"You're such an idiot," I said to myself, remembering that first day in the ER when Alex took off his shirt to impress me.

My instincts had told me that he was a player. Maybe I should have trusted them.

$\backsim$

By the time I arrived home, I was spitting mad. Mad at Alex for playing me, and mad at myself for becoming so ridiculously infatuated that I believed our relationship was actually going somewhere.

I'd always been a proud and independent person, and the last thing I wanted to do was fall apart over a guy, so as soon as I walked through the door and removed my coat, I pulled out my cell phone and texted him a message:

Hi Alex. I don't think this is going to work out. I can't come for dinner tonight. Sorry.

Before I had a chance to think it through or craft a gentler message, I impulsively pressed send and tossed the phone onto the kitchen counter.

"There!" I shouted at the touch screen. "How do you like *them* apples!"

The phone immediately vibrated back at me with an incoming call.

"Oh, crap," I whispered, and picked it up. I swiped the screen to answer it. "Hello?"

"Hi," Alex said. There was a gentleness in his tone. He spoke to me carefully, as if I stood on a tenth-floor window ledge. "I just got your text."

I shut my eyes and scrunched my nose. Maybe I'd been a bit too trigger happy sending that message.

"Yeah, well…" I sat down at the kitchen table. "I'm sorry to break our date like that…in a text. I should have called to do it."

"To do *what* exactly?" he asked. "I'm confused. You said you didn't think it was going to work out. Are you breaking up with me?"

"Breaking up…" My eyebrows lifted. "I think…maybe that's overstating it a bit. That implies we're actually a couple, and I don't think we were quite there."

Otherwise he wouldn't have invited his *other* girlfriend over to keep him entertained on a rainy afternoon.

Alex was quiet for a long moment.

"I thought we were," he finally said. "I don't understand, Audrey. I'm disappointed. I was looking forward to seeing you tonight."

"I'm sure you'll get over it," I harshly replied, wondering if Melanie was still there and he was talking to me from behind his bathroom door.

Playing us both.

"What's wrong?" he asked. "Something must have happened because you don't sound like yourself."

I stood and paced around the kitchen while sparks of heat flashed through my body. "Okay then. If you really want to know...I came by your place earlier today and saw whose car was parked out front."

My explanation was met with complete silence.

"Did you hear what I said?" I asked.

"Yeah, I heard you," he replied, "but it's not what you think. Why don't you come over here so we can talk about it? Let me explain."

All those clichéd responses made me want to laugh bitterly into the phone, but I couldn't because I was overcome by a sudden melancholy. I'd had such high hopes for this relationship. I'd been wildly attracted to Alex from the get-go and I honestly believed we were falling in love.

"I don't think so," I replied—because I didn't want to prolong the agony. I may have been heartbroken, but I still had my dignity.

"Then let's talk about it *now*," he suggested. "I didn't invite Melanie over. She just showed up at my door in tears and I had no choice. I had to invite her in. She was a mess."

Part of me wanted desperately to hear more, but another part was afraid to listen. I didn't know if I could trust him.

I didn't say anything in reply, but he nevertheless soldiered on. "She doesn't want it to be over and she came over here begging me for another chance. I felt bad, but I told her we were done. I spent almost two hours trying to convince her that she was going to be okay and that she'd find someone else. It was exhausting. Then as soon as she left, I got your text."

I went into the living room and sank down onto the sofa. "Did you tell her about me?" I asked.

"Of course," he replied. Then he paused. "I never saw anyone cry like that. She sobbed and begged and pleaded. It was rough."

I covered my eyes with a hand. "I'm sorry for sending the text. I was angry."

He didn't say anything for a minute or two. "I suppose it must have looked pretty bad when you saw her car parked out front, but I just couldn't bring myself to slam the door in her face."

"You're a nice person," I said with a sigh. "Compassionate." It was a quality I admired.

"Does that mean we're still on for dinner?" he carefully asked. "And I warn you, if you say no…I might show up at *your* house in tears, begging and pleading."

After a long pause, I smiled. "I'll come by in an hour. We can talk more about everything tonight."

"Good," he replied. "I'll see you then."

I ended the call and flopped back onto the sofa, more relieved than I cared to admit that we would still be having dinner that night.

My relief was to be short-lived, however, because something else was about to happen. I didn't know it then, but all of this was the beginning of a nightmare that would take quite a bit of time to resolve.

Over dinner that night, Alex explained everything that happened with Melanie that afternoon, and he also held nothing back about their intense six-month relationship.

From very early on, he had recognized she wasn't completely stable. She was jealous and often shouted, ranted and threw things—but he continued to date her, admitting that he was attracted to her physically. She had a way of smiling and making up for everything with a pouty look and a seductive flip of her hair.

"It was a good learning experience," he said as we lingered over coffee, "because I won't make that mistake again. Now I know what I want."

"And what's that?" I asked.

"I want to marry a girl with a good head on her shoulders. Smart and sensible. Someone who will be a good mother. Someone rational and kind."

The fact that he would even *mention* wanting marriage someday caught me off guard, and my heart melted.

"All good qualities," I replied, setting down my coffee mug. "But don't forget integrity. When it comes to marriage, fidelity is key. That's what my dad always used to say."

Alex leaned back in his chair and stared at me across the table for a long moment. "I'm glad you didn't dump me today."

"I'm glad, too," I softly replied as my heart pounded with excitement. Then Alex paid the bill and we left.

Alex invited me up to his apartment, but I didn't stay long because I had to work at seven the next morning. When it was time to go, I had to tear myself away from him on the sofa. Then I kissed him for another ten minutes at the door before I headed home.

As I drove through the city, I listened to the hit parade on the radio, tapped my fingers on the steering wheel and felt positively euphoric. When I pulled into my driveway, however, my blissful mood veered sharply downward and anxiety spiked in my veins.

It looked like a bomb had gone off in my yard.

This time I couldn't blame it on the raccoons. Clearly, someone had ripped open the garbage bags around the side of the house and spread everything all over the grass. Dirty tissues, wrappers and rotten food items were strewn from one corner to the other. The bins were over on their sides on the front walk.

I shut off the car engine and sat motionless, staring, then reached for my phone and called Alex to tell him what happened before I dialed the police.

To make a long story short, the cops put two and two together and paid a visit to Melanie the following morning to question her about the garbage on my lawn and my suspicious open window a week earlier. Naturally she denied any knowledge of those things.

The officers filed a report regardless, but it didn't end there. Later that day, as I walked out of the hospital after work, I spotted her from a distance in the glare of the sun. She was leaning against the driver's side door of my Mustang, filing her fingernails.

I stopped and moved behind a pillar at the entrance. Digging into my purse, I called Alex.

"Hey there," he said.

"Hi, it's me," I replied. "You're not going to believe this. I just got off work and Melanie is here. She's waiting by my car. What should I do? Should I go talk to her or call the cops?"

He let out a groan. "Oh God, Audrey, I'm so sorry. You shouldn't have to deal with this. It's my fault."

"No, it's not. You can't help that she's a nutcase. What do you think she wants?"

He sighed with resignation. "She probably wants to talk to you about the cops coming over to her place this morning."

"Maybe she wants to apologize," I suggested optimistically.

"Not likely. Listen, don't believe anything she says, all right? She might lie to you about me."

"What would she say?"

"I don't know...that I invited her over yesterday. Or that we kissed."

I peered out from behind the pillar to watch her. "*Did* you kiss?"

He hesitated, and my stomach turned over with dread. "I kissed her on the cheek a few times," he replied. "I was trying to comfort her, to get her to stop crying."

I didn't want to doubt his rendition, but there was still a part of me that wasn't sure.

Either way, I had to walk to my car eventually.

"I'm going to see what she wants," I firmly said, starting off toward the parking lot. "I'll call you later."

She must have sensed my approach because when I was still a fair distance away, she looked up, pushed away from my vehicle and shoved the emery board into her brown leather purse.

As I drew near, her gaze narrowed and I braced myself for an uncomfortable confrontation.

"What are you doing here, Melanie?" I asked, stopping in front of the grill of my Mustang. The sunlight reflected off the shiny steel and nearly blinded me.

"Waiting for you," she replied.

"Why?"

"Because there's something we need to talk about."

Arranging my keys between each of my fingers, I gripped them tightly and said, "What would that be?"

"Don't act all innocent." She strode closer but I held my ground—though she was at least six inches taller than me. "You sent the cops to my house this morning. I think that creates a problem."

"What creates a problem is when you come over to *my* house and dump garbage all over my lawn."

Melanie pushed her sunglasses further up the bridge of her tiny upturned nose. "I never did that."

"No? I think you did. I also think you broke into my house last week."

She scoffed. "You're nuts! Why would I do that?"

"I don't know," I replied, shrugging. "Maybe because you're upset that I'm dating Alex."

She folded her arms across her chest. "If you had any brains in your head, you wouldn't waste your time on him, and you'd see that I'm doing you a favor by coming here."

"How?" I asked with disbelief.

"Because I'm giving you fair warning that he'll break your heart—just like he broke mine. He's a player."

I brushed by her to unlock my car door. "I appreciate the advice, but I'll take my chances."

"Are you dense?" she asked, following. "He's not worth your time. The only reason he's into you is because you weren't interested, so you were a challenge. He'll say anything to make you fall for him, and as soon as you do, he'll get bored and move on. Mark my words. That's what he does."

These were not words I wanted to hear because I hadn't felt this happy in years, and I didn't even want to *think* about my relationship with Alex coming to an end.

This was crazy; I shouldn't *have* to think about it—because I knew Melanie wasn't rational. I'd be a fool to trust anything she said. I willed myself not to listen.

Shoving my key into the lock, I opened my door. Before I got in, however, I said one last thing: "What I do with my life is none of your business, and if you ever set foot on my property again, I'll have the cops at your door so fast, your head will spin."

As I was sliding into the driver's seat, she moved around the front of my car and grabbed hold of the door to prevent me from closing it.

"I'm just trying to help you," she said with teeth clenched tight.

I tugged at the door but she gripped it hard. "Let go!"

At last Melanie stepped back. I violently slammed the door. With shaking hands, I turned the key in the ignition. The engine revved and I hit the gas.

My tires squealed as I sped out of the parking lot. I must have checked my rearview mirror at least twenty times on the way home.

—⟶

"Do you think I have enough evidence to file a restraining order?" I asked Cathy when we met for spinning class that night.

"I don't know," she replied. "Did you tell the police she was waiting for you after work?"

"Yes, I called them right away, told them every word she said and they added it to the report."

Cathy tied her hair back in a ponytail. "The fact that she knew what time you were getting off work is kind of creepy. I'm glad you have a written record of everything, just in case."

"In case of *what*?" I asked with more than a little concern as I climbed onto a stationary bike and adjusted my feet on the pedals. "You don't think she'd do anything *really* crazy, do you?"

Cathy mounted the bike beside me. "It's hard to say, but she definitely seems to have stalker-brain. She must really be obsessed with Alex."

"I can hardly blame her," I found myself saying. "He's pretty amazing."

"Maybe so." Cathy leaned forward and grasped the handlebars. "But that doesn't make it okay to dump garbage on someone's lawn. And are you sure you can trust Alex? What was he doing with a girl like that in the first place? You said he was with her for six months."

"He admits he was dazzled by her beauty, but he regrets it now," I replied in his defense.

Cathy sighed. "I guess a lot of people end up regretting past relationships. Just be careful, all right?"

"I will," I replied as the instructor walked into the studio and turned on the music.

In all honesty, I didn't believe Melanie would do anything legitimately dangerous. She was just angry because her pride was bruised. She looked like a supermodel and probably couldn't believe a brainy little nurse with glasses had stolen her boyfriend.

The cops had already knocked on her door and delivered a warning. A report had been filed. If anything happened to me, she'd be the number one suspect.

Surely she wouldn't be that stupid.

As it turned out, Melanie *was* that stupid.

Maybe I was a little stupid, too, in assuming she wasn't dangerous…

After I left my spinning class, I drove to Alex's place and picked him up for a movie. Later, he invited me up to his apartment, but I said no because I had to be at work at 7:00 the next morning. Besides, things were heating up between us and I knew that if I gave in, I might stay all night, and I wasn't ready for that.

Especially with Melanie still in the picture.

Though I told myself she wasn't rational—and surely everything she said about Alex was a lie—I still had my doubts. Maybe I was overly cautious. Maybe a part of me believed that a guy as gorgeous as Alex couldn't possibly be the type to settle down—not when beautiful women would always be throwing themselves at him.

So when it came time to say goodnight, Alex gave me a kiss and got out of the car, still limping on his good foot. He stood under the streetlamp in a leather jacket and jeans, smiling down at me.

"Call me from work tomorrow?" he asked.

"I will."

Pulling away from the curb, I left him standing on the sidewalk.

When I arrived home, I was at least pleased to find my front lawn free of spilled garbage. Gathering up my purse and keys, I strode to my front door.

There wasn't a single breath of wind in the air as I fiddled with my keys in the dark, wishing I'd left my porch light on.

When at last I found the right key, I let myself in and flicked on the lights.

The silence inside was rather ominous and I found myself hesitant to move from my spot on the welcome mat.

I really should get a dog, I thought. To be greeted at the door by a live creature with a wagging tail would be far preferable to this fear and uncertainty, especially when I might be dealing with a potential stalker.

I tried self-talk. *Don't be paranoid. All the windows and doors were locked when you left. There's no one here.*

Taking a deep breath, I moved into the living room and turned on a couple of lamps and the television. Then I went to the kitchen and flicked on the overhead light.

The window near the back door was shut tight and the blinds were closed, which gave me some peace of mind. Nevertheless, I moved from room to room, turning on lights and checking behind closet doors.

Nothing seemed out of order, so I changed into my pajamas and planted myself on the sofa to watch some TV.

The sound of my cell phone ringing woke me shortly before 5:00 a.m. At first I thought I was having some kind of lucid dream because I also heard sirens and it seemed very real. The phone rang four times, stopped for a moment, then resumed ringing again.

Confused and disoriented, I sat up and squinted through the darkness. Just as I was about to answer the phone, there was a loud, aggressive banging at my front door—and I knew that part wasn't a dream. My belly exploded with panic and I scrambled to pick up the phone.

"Hello?"

"Audrey, it's Alex. You have to get out of the house."

Sparks of adrenaline lit in my veins. Tossing the covers aside, I sat up on the edge of the bed and flicked on the light. "What are you talking about?"

The thunderous banging at the front door continued, more insistently, sending me into a blinding state of red-hot terror.

"There's someone at my door!"

"Your house is on fire," Alex said. "David just called me. He should be outside right now with a truck."

Only then did I notice smoke wafting into my bedroom from under the closed door. "Oh, my God." I leapt to my feet. "I see smoke."

"Get out of there," he said. "Can you go out the back window?"

I turned to look at it. "Yes."

"Do it now."

Without bothering to put on a bathrobe or slippers, I hurried around the bed, unlocked the window and shoved it fully open. The next thing I knew I was sliding clumsily over the sill and falling onto the prickly rosebush below. The thorns tore through my pajamas and scratched the flesh on my arms, legs and face.

"Ouch!"

Still clutching my phone, I spoke to Alex. "I'm okay. I'm outside now." I crawled out of the garden onto the damp, cool grass, then rose to my feet and turned around. "Holy crap!"

The kitchen windows were aglow, flickering with orange-colored flames inside. "The house really is on fire!"

"Go around front and tell them you're okay," Alex said. "Is there anyone else inside?"

"No," I replied, beginning to shake from shock as I ran around the side of the house.

When I reached the driveway, two fire trucks were parked out front and a third tanker was turning onto the street. Lights flashed and a couple of firefighters were dragging hoses across my lawn.

My house is burning. With everything I own inside of it.

I waved my hands at them. "I'm here!" I shouted. "I'm the owner!"

Glancing at the front door, I noticed it had already been broken down. I assumed someone must have gone inside to rescue me.

A fireman approached. He wore a coat with reflective stripes, an air tank strapped to his back, a helmet and facemask. "Is there anyone else inside?" he asked over the roar of the engines. An ambulance pulled up just then.

Giant plumes of black, billowing smoke rose up from the burning roof. I heard glass smashing, the snap and crackle of the flames.

"No, it's just me," I told him. "There's no one else."

"Are you hurt?"

His gaze swept over my face with concern. I glanced down at my trembling hands and realized I was scratched and bleeding from the rose bush thorns.

"I'm fine," I said. "I did this when I climbed out the window."

He laid a gloved hand on the small of my back and guided me further away from the house. "Come this way."

I followed him in a daze as he led me toward the paramedic who was just hopping out of the ambulance.

"This is the homeowner," the firefighter said. "She climbed out the back window."

The paramedic opened the rear doors of the ambulance, fetched a blanket and quickly wrapped it around me. "You were lucky to get out of there," she said. "It looks pretty bad."

I glanced back and realized the firefighter had left me. He was now speaking to one of the others, no doubt letting them know there were no other people inside.

Oh God, my house. Would they be able to save it? To save anything?

And how did it start? Had Melanie done this?

Fifteen

ust as the paramedic finished cleaning all the bloody cuts on my face and arms, a cab turned onto my street. A police officer waved his arms to prevent it from crossing the barricades. It pulled to a halt and Alex hopped out of the back. He spoke to the officer who immediately let him through, then looked up at my house, now entirely engulfed in flames.

"Alex!" I called.

He heard my voice and limped toward me. Still wrapped in the woolen blanket, I hurried to meet him.

"Thank God you're all right," he said, pulling me into his arms.

"I'm fine, but I haven't seen David at all," I said. "They've been keeping me here, well out of the way."

Alex watched a firefighter spray water through the broken living room window while another dragged a hose through the front door. "Do you have any idea how it started?" he asked.

"None," I replied. "I was sound asleep when you called—and thank God you did or I might not be talking to you right now. But how did you know?"

"One of your neighbors saw the flames and called 911," he explained. "As soon as David realized it was your house, he called me."

We stood together, watching the scene unfold. By now the fire had spread through the entire house and flames were spiking out through the roof. I'd never seen so much smoke in my life. The sound of the fire crackling, timbers snapping and breaking was deafening as the roof collapsed before my eyes. I knew more engines were on their way because I could hear more sirens in the distance. A cop was speaking through a megaphone to a crowd that had gathered to watch.

"Will they be able to save anything?" I asked, already knowing the answer but not wanting to face it.

"Not likely," Alex replied. "I hope you have good insurance."

"I do, but I only bought the house last year. It's mortgaged to the hilt. There's hardly any equity. I'll have to start from scratch."

He put his arm around me and I rested my head on his shoulder. "Everything will be okay," he said. "You're alive. That's all that matters."

A police officer approached us. I stepped back and wiped a tear from my cheek.

"Are you the homeowner?" he asked.

"Yes," I replied, hugging the blanket tighter around my shoulders. "My name is Audrey Livingston."

He held a notepad and pen, and seemed eager to write something down. "Do you have any idea how the fire started?"

"No, I was asleep with the bedroom door closed. One of my neighbors saw the flames and called 911. I don't know which neighbor it was."

"Were you using the stove last night?" he asked. "Any chance you might have left a curling iron on? Are you a smoker?"

"No to all those questions," I replied. "I was out for the evening and when I came home around midnight, I watched a little

TV, but that was it. Then I turned off all the lights and went to bed."

He wrote that down, and I glanced uneasily at Alex.

"I don't want to make false accusations," I said, "because I don't have any proof, but I've had a few run-ins with a woman who doesn't like me very much. I'm not sure if she's capable of something like this, but if there's any chance it might be arson, she could be a suspect. There's been a report filed about her." I looked up at Alex. "I'm sorry."

"Don't apologize to *me*," he said. "I don't know if she's capable of this either, but if she did do it, we need to know."

The cop questioned me further about the report I'd filed, then asked if I had a place to stay, because obviously I couldn't go back to my house.

"You can come home with me," Alex offered, "and stay as long as you need to."

"Thanks," I replied, not wanting to sound ungrateful, but I felt as if, since the day I met him, my whole life had begun to spiral out of control.

Strange as it may seem for me to say this, there would come a day when I would want to thank Melanie Wilder for setting fire to my house.

Yes, she had done it. The fire department had confirmed it was arson, and the police found enough evidence on the scene and in Melanie's apartment to charge her with arson and attempted murder.

It was also revealed to us that she had been convicted previously for assault. At the age of sixteen she beat a girl unconscious with a baseball bat—because the girl had been texting Melanie's boyfriend.

Under the advice of her lawyer, Melanie confessed to setting fire to my house, was later found guilty and sentenced to eight years in a mental health facility.

But why would I ever thank Melanie for destroying everything I owned and nearly killing me in the process?

Because if it hadn't been for her, I might not be where I am today.

On the morning my house burned down—after I finished answering questions and there was nothing left for me to do on the scene—I went with Alex to his apartment.

At first I was hesitant about staying with him and suggested I go to my friend Cathy's place to wait for my insurance to come through. Cathy had already left for work that morning, however, and Alex was persistent about not leaving me alone. And I *did* want to be with him. He was knowledgeable about everything related to the fire and he made me feel safe. He was attentive and devoted—partly, I suspected, because he felt guilty for bringing Melanie into my life.

Since I had nothing but my cell phone and the pajamas I was wearing, he took me shopping for clothes and shoes and sundry items like shampoo and a toothbrush.

Though I felt lucky to be alive, I couldn't stop crying—not only because I'd nearly died in that fire, but I lost irreplaceable treasures that day. Everything I owned was gone, including my purse, credit cards and passport. My photo albums and all my favorite books and DVDs were burned to a crisp. I'd just bought an expensive down comforter for my bed, which I loved. That, too, was gone. My laptop with all my files and videos no longer existed.

Alex was there for me emotionally and held me close that night when I woke up imagining that I smelled smoke. I was concerned because his apartment was on the third floor. How would we escape if the building was burning from the bottom up?

He reminded me that Melanie was in custody, so she could no longer try to hurt me.

"What if someone downstairs is smoking in bed?" I asked.

He showed me the fire escape and tested the batteries in all the smoke alarms. He also went downstairs to check for fire in the stairwells, then ventured outside with a flashlight to look over the exterior of the building.

All this, he did simply to ease my mind. When he came back upstairs he held me close and kissed my forehead, gently stroked my hair. "You're safe here," he whispered until I fell asleep.

I did feel safe and protected, and for that reason I chose to stay with him—at least temporarily—until I got my affairs in order.

Little did I know it was a choice that would affect the rest my life.

⸙

"It's been two and a half months," Cathy said to me as we walked through the mall on a Saturday morning licking ice cream cones. "Don't get me wrong, I really like Alex, but is this what you want? You always said you'd never live with a guy. That you'd want to be married first."

As it happened, I'd received my insurance settlement not long after the fire, which had taken care of my mortgage. There was still a fair chunk of change left over from the value of my furniture and belongings—enough for a modest down payment on a new house—so I had no excuse not to be back out on my own by then.

"I did say that," I replied, "but whenever I think about living alone again and coming home to an empty house at night, I want to crawl into a cupboard."

Cathy linked her arm through mine. "I'm sure that's a normal reaction after what you've been through, but you could get a roommate or a dog. And you know you're always welcome at my place. There's a spare bedroom in the basement. Bob and I would love to have you stay with us for as long as you need to."

I bit into my waffle cone and gave her a sidelong glance. "Do you think I'm making a mistake, staying with Alex?"

She took a moment to form a reply. "No. Like I said, I think he's a good guy. It's just that…you barely knew him when Melanie burned your house down. You'd only been dating a couple of weeks. Now suddenly you're living together. I just don't want you to drift along and end up getting hurt."

I was unnerved by her choice of words because I'd always been a top student at school and had pursued my nursing career with relentless ambition. No one had ever accused me of *drifting*.

This made me lose my appetite. I approached a garbage can and tossed away what was left of my waffle cone.

"Sometimes it *does* feel like we're just playing house," I admitted at last.

"How so?"

I buried my hands in my jacket pockets. "Well…We never actually discussed the idea of living together or making a serious commitment. So I guess I'm not entirely sure what's going on between us. Are we a couple? I honestly don't know the answer to that question. I wish I did."

Cathy considered everything. "What do you think he would do if you told him you were going to start looking for your own place? If you thanked him for letting you stay with him, but said it was time for you to get back on your own two feet, would he say, 'You're welcome, Audrey. It was no trouble at all. Let me know how I can help.' Or would he be devastated and beg you to stay?"

Cathy and I stepped onto the escalator. "I have no idea what he would do."

"What would you *want* him to do?" she asked.

"I don't know. Beg me to stay, I guess."

She laughed softly. "That doesn't sound very convincing."

We reached the second floor and stepped off the escalator. "Let me ask you this," Cathy said. "Are you in love with him?"

We walked slowly past a crowd of teenagers. "I'm not sure. I think I'm *afraid* to say yes."

"Why?"

"Because I'm not sure I could ever trust him to be the kind of man I'd want to marry."

"Why not?"

I gazed at the fashionable, faceless mannequins in the storefront windows as we passed by. "He can be a real flirt sometimes. Beautiful women will always be batting their eyelashes at him and that can be tempting, lead to indiscretions. I don't want to be the ball and chain who waits for him at home."

"If this is because of Melanie," Cathy interrupted, "don't forget she was a nutcase. Whatever she said to you, you can't trust it. It shouldn't affect how you feel about him."

"It's not just that," I replied. "It's my own gut feeling. Remember that first day when I met him in the ER? I told myself to stay away from him. I believed he was a player before I ever met Melanie."

"But do you still feel that way?" she asked. "Even after living with him for two months?"

I considered the question carefully. "I don't know, and I don't know how he feels either."

"Then you should talk to him about it. If you're uncomfortable asking him point blank where your relationship is going, you could always lead with 'I should probably find a place of my own,' and see how he responds."

"That's brilliant," I said. "It's a clever way to feel him out. I'll do it tonight."

A fter I said good-bye to Cathy at the mall, I went to the supermarket to pick up ingredients for a special dinner I planned to cook for Alex. His favorite meal was lasagna with Caesar salad, so I spent the afternoon slicing, dicing and stirring tomato sauce in his apartment.

As I began to layer the sauce over the noodles and cheese, however, I found myself swallowing back the urge to gag.

Eventually unable to continue, I dropped the spoon onto the counter, which splattered sauce everywhere, and hurried to the living room to escape the smells of the kitchen. I pressed the back of my hand to my nose and stood for a moment, heart racing, fearing I might vomit.

Thankfully the sensation passed, but I felt a little light-headed, so I sat down on the sofa and put my head between my knees. I sat in that position for a long time.

"Please, God, don't let me be pregnant," I whispered.

A few minutes later, I was able to stand up.

Not being the type of person to stick my head in the sand or worry about things that might never happen, I grabbed my purse, left the unfinished lasagna on the counter and ran down to the pharmacy to buy a test.

An hour later, I finished preparing the lasagna. I slid it into the oven and it was fully cooked by the time Alex walked in the door.

"Smells great in here," he said, shrugging out of his jacket and tossing it onto the chair. He was out of his cast now, so he moved into the kitchen with ease, noticed the lasagna on the stove and the salad bowl sitting on the table next to a bottle of wine.

He then found me lying on the sofa.

"Did you have a good day?" he asked, bending to kiss me on the cheek.

I rose slowly to my feet. "It was interesting," I replied. "Are you hungry?"

"You know me. I'm always hungry."

"Then let's eat." With an uneasy wave of apprehension, I followed Alex into the kitchen, served up two plates and carried them to the table.

He picked up the bottle of wine and poured us each a glass. I didn't offer any objection, though I didn't touch mine.

"I'm glad you're home," I said, "because I need to talk to you about something."

He looked at me uncertainly. "Okay."

As I recalled my conversation with Cathy earlier that day, I wasn't sure how to begin. In the end, I settled with this: "I've been thinking…It's probably time I started looking for my own place."

To this day, I still wonder why I opened with that statement. Was I testing him? Yes, I suppose I was.

He set down his fork and leaned back in his chair. "There's no hurry."

"I know," I cheerfully replied. "You've been really great about letting me stay here. I appreciate it, but we both know I should have my own place."

"But *why?*" he asked, as if it was an insane prospect to even consider.

"Because…" I shifted uncomfortably in my chair. "To be honest, I'm not really sure what's going on here. We were barely dating a couple of weeks before I made this my home—which was supposed to be temporary."

I paused to gather my thoughts, because I didn't want to play games with him, but I needed to know how he felt about our relationship.

I set my fork down as well. "If you really want to know," I said, "I never imagined myself living with someone. I'm kind of old fashioned that way. I always thought I'd be married first. It's kind of crazy that we're here like this, eating dinner together every night, waking up in the same bed each morning."

His brow furrowed with concern. "You're not happy?"

My heart squeezed with regret because I didn't want to hurt him. He'd been kind to me, and whatever doubts I had about his ability to be faithful were my own. He'd never actually done anything to suggest he was running around on me. At least not at this point.

"Of course I'm happy," I said. "I love being with you. But don't you think we're moving too fast? Honestly, I thought I'd be staying with you for a few days, but here we are after two months. I'm not sure either of us knew what we were getting into."

"Maybe not at the time," he argued, "but does it really matter? Now that you're here, I don't want you to go. I like what we have."

How much do you like it? I wondered. *And for how long will you want it?*

He raked a hand through his hair. "Please don't move out," he said. "Stay with me."

I couldn't seem to move or form words. He was saying all the things I'd hoped he would say, yet I still didn't feel confident that this was true love—the forever kind. *Was he a forever kind of guy? Was it even possible to know something like that about a person in such a short amount of time?*

Slowly I pushed my chair back, stood up and moved to the kitchen. Alex followed.

"What's wrong?" he said. "You're not yourself. Did I do something wrong? If I did, please tell me."

Now I felt like a heel.

Turning to face him, I wrapped my arms around his neck, rose up on my tiptoes and pulled him close. "You didn't do anything wrong. I'm happy, but something's changed and I don't know how I'm going to explain it."

He held me away so he could look into my eyes. "What is it?"

I shook my head. "You're not going to want to hear this."

"Let me decide that," he insisted.

"Okay then…" Taking a deep breath, I spoke candidly. "I'm pregnant."

Alex just stared at me. "Are you sure?"

I nodded my head. "I felt sick this afternoon so I took a test and the result was positive. A positive result is ninety-nine percent accurate, so yes, I'm sure."

He backed away and leaned against the counter. "Wow."

I moved to stand beside him and leaned against the counter as well. "Tell me about it. I thought I was going to pass out when

I read the result. I'm really sorry. I thought we were being careful. Please believe me—I didn't plan this."

He reached for my hand, raised it to his lips and kissed it. "I believe you, and I'm not sorry, because I nearly had a heart attack just now when you said you wanted to move out. Were you just trying to let me off the hook or something?"

I looked down at my shoes. "I guess I just needed to know where we stood. How you felt about me."

"So you were testing me?"

I nodded.

He turned to face me, cradled my chin in his hand and lifted my face, forcing me to meet his gaze. "How could you not know how I feel?"

I shrugged and lowered my gaze. He bent at the knees to place himself in my line of vision.

"I love you, Audrey," he said, "and I'm not letting you go. If you're pregnant, I want to marry you."

My eyes nearly bugged out of my head. "Are you insane? We barely know each other."

"That's not true," he argued. "We've spent a lot of time together, been through some rough situations, and hell, when you know, you know. I knew it the first moment I laid eyes on you in the ER. That was it for me. There was no getting you out of my head, and now that I have you, I don't want to lose you. Not ever. I love what we have, so let's just get married."

I don't know why I had such a hard time believing all the lovely things he said to me. Did I not consider myself worthy of such passion? Did I still believe he was just a charmer and a cheat? Had I not yet lowered my shields?

"I'm not sure about this," I said. "We're talking about the rest of our lives. Maybe we should think about it and not rush into anything."

The heartbreak I saw in his eyes made my chest hurt. *What was wrong with me? Why couldn't I just say yes to his proposal, step into his arms and weep tears of joy?* It should have been a magical moment we'd remember forever, but I'd spoiled it.

And I didn't stop there.

"If you don't mind," I said, backing away, "I think I'll stay at Cathy's tonight."

Alex's eyebrows pulled together in a frown. "You don't need to do that."

"I know, but I want to give you some space to think about this."

"I don't need space," he firmly told me.

"But I do," I replied. "This is all happening way too fast, Alex. I need time to process it."

I felt a mad impulse to flee out the door.

Moving past him, I grabbed my purse and keys from the hall table.

He followed me. "Don't go," he said.

My stomach careened with uncertainty. *Why was I doing this? Was I still testing him, or was I unsure of my own feelings? Did I not love him?*

If I *did* love him, shouldn't this be easier?

Turning around, I hugged him. "I don't mean to be cruel. It's only until tomorrow, until I figure this out."

With that, he let me go.

Nineteen

The next day was pure torture—not only because I was confused and unsure about my future with Alex, but because I felt nauseous.

The soda crackers were no help at all and the smells in the hospital made me gag.

I made an appointment to see my doctor at the end of the week—with the hope that he could prescribe something to help with the nausea—but otherwise, I felt as if I was floating in limbo.

I was lying face down with my eyes closed in Cathy's spare bedroom in the basement, missing Alex, when a knock sounded at the door. "Ugh…" I replied.

The door opened and Cathy peered in. "You have a visitor."

I lifted my head. "Is it Alex?"

"Yes."

Despite the powerful temptation to remain in bed and not move a muscle, I sat up and swung my legs to the floor. "I should talk to him. He deserves that."

"Yes he does," Cathy replied with a hint of scolding in her tone.

I'd told her everything about my conversation with Alex the night before, so when I stood up and met her in the doorway, she took my face in her hands. "What is wrong with your brain? He passed your test with flying colors last night, then he *proposed*. Why are you even here when you should be with *him*, making wedding plans?"

I stared at her in a fog of self-doubt. "We've only known each other for two months. I need more time to test the waters."

She dropped her hands to her side. "That sort of makes sense, but I still think you're afraid to trust him, and the only reason is because he's so good looking, which is very superficial of you. Beauty is only skin deep, you know."

We climbed the stairs together.

"It's not fair to him," she continued, following me up. "You're judging him based on his looks when he's been nothing but loyal and devoted since the day you met."

Reaching the top, I stopped and turned. "I've always been overly cautious. Do you know I looked at thirty houses before I made an offer on mine? And then I visited four different banks to make sure I got the best interest rate. And when you guys decided to take a year off after high school and travel to Europe, I wouldn't even consider that. I had to make sure I had my future locked down. Maybe I *do* have a problem."

Cathy closed the door to the basement. "You're very practical, which isn't a bad thing. It's one of the things Alex likes about you."

"Well," I said, waving my hands through the air, "people shouldn't go around blindly leaping about. It's more sensible to make informed decisions."

"Yes, that's true," Cathy agreed, "if you're buying a new car or a fridge. But when it comes to relationships there's only so much you can know about the future. Alex could get hit by a bus a year from now and you'd still end up heartbroken. But at this moment in time, what you *do* know is that you're having a baby together and he's a good guy. He wants to do the right thing and marry you, and don't try to tell me you're not in love with him because I know you are. I've never seen you so happy. You're just afraid to admit you love him because you're afraid you might lose him someday."

I looked down at the floor.

"Let me ask you this…" Cathy said. "We both know he'll be a great dad and a good provider. If I had a crystal ball and I could tell you for sure that he would never cheat on you, would you marry him?"

I glanced toward the front door. "Yes, but there's no such thing as a crystal ball, so I still feel like I'm flying blind."

But isn't that the point of living? To go out there and experience things, to explore and actually *learn* something? Isn't that how we grow?

Alex had come for me in the Buick. It was parked across the street with the windows rolled down—there was no air-conditioning—so he was sitting in the rocking chair on Cathy's front porch.

"Hey gorgeous, want to go cruisin'?" he asked with a smile.

I looked down at him and was instantly captivated. There were butterflies. Goose bumps. You name it. The whole nine yards.

"Sure," I replied with a chuckle. "Let me grab my purse."

A few minutes later we were driving around town with the radio on.

"I just want you to know," Alex said, "I did want to give you some space tonight, but in the end I couldn't do it. I hate being away from you, and I couldn't take not knowing if you were ever coming back."

"I'm sorry," I replied. "I know I left in a hurry last night. I was frazzled."

"Are you still frazzled?" he asked, glancing across at me.

I was locked in his gaze—I felt safe and cared for—and I didn't want to leave it.

"Less so now," I replied. "I missed you last night."

"I missed you, too."

As I watched him handle the car while we listened to music on the radio, all my usual fears and doubts seemed to fade into the background. Maybe I just needed a good swift kick in the butt, and Cathy had handled that task quite capably.

Sticking my arm out the window, I used the flat of my hand to surf on the wind.

"This car is something else," I said. "There's just something special about her."

"I'm glad you think so."

As we drove down Main Street, pedestrians stopped to stare. Parents pointed, probably explaining to their children that it was a rare old car. Other drivers honked and waved.

"How often do you take her out on the main roads?" I asked.

"Not often," he replied. "Only on special occasions."

"Is that what this is?" I asked.

He slid a glance at me. "Last night you told me you're pregnant with my child. I think that qualifies." He turned onto Center Street. "Want to go for a walk? There's something I want to show you."

Naturally I said yes, so he took us to Wickham Park.

CHAPTER

Twenty

ෙ෴

"Is this what you wanted to show me?" I asked as we stopped to look over the rail of the white arched bridge at the pond. "Because I've been here before, you know."

"I figured you had," he replied. "And no, it's not what I wanted to show you. First we need to do some talking."

A flock of birds startled at something and took flight from the top branches of an oak tree in the forest. I jumped and laid a hand over my heart. "That scared me."

Alex looked up, then he turned to lean over the bridge rail and looked down at the water. "Everything about this day is scary."

"Why?" I asked.

He met my gaze. "Because I woke up not knowing how you feel or what you want. I know what *I* want, but you…? You're a mystery."

"I don't mean to be," I replied. "I'm just being careful. I don't want to get hurt."

"Why do you think you'll get hurt?"

"Because…" I paused and looked down at a duck swimming slowly under the bridge beneath us. "Do you remember the first day we met? You came on to me pretty aggressively and I thought you were a playboy. Then I found out you had a girlfriend, which didn't exactly convince me that you were a one-woman kind of man."

"How many times do I have to say it? She wasn't my girlfriend."

"But she *was*, before that. Obviously she still wanted to be, but you were ready to move on. How long until you'll want to move on from me and this baby?"

He frowned. "That will never happen because I want to marry you. We'll be a family and that will be that."

I sighed. "You sound confident."

"I am."

Yet I was still unsure, still unable to take that leap of faith and believe wholeheartedly that everything would work out, that our lives would be filled with roses and sunshine. I had a troubling feeling of dread that I simply couldn't explain or escape. I would understand that feeling later, of course, but in that moment, it was a mystery to me.

"Audrey," he said, taking hold of my hand. "I lost my father when I was nine, and I remember how awful it was because I loved him a lot. I would never wish that on my children. I'll want to be there for them every day, forever, and I want to be there for you, too. Family is everything to me and you need to believe that. You need to believe in *me*."

All the muscles in my body turned warm. Laying my hand on his cheek, I said, "I do believe in you."

He leaned closer and pressed his lips to mine. My legs turned to jelly, then he surprised me by getting down on one knee and pulling out a small white box.

Gazing up at me with steady, smiling eyes, he opened the box to reveal a stunning diamond solitaire ring. I gasped and covered my mouth with a hand.

"I love you," he said, "and I want to marry you so that we can be a family, together forever. I promise I'll do everything in my power to make you happy. I'll be faithful, Audrey—*to you and only you*—until the day I die."

A tear slid down my cheek because in that shimmering moment on that beautiful white bridge in the park, I was so madly in love, I could barely see straight.

And I believed him. I believed him with every breath I took.

Fire

After a month-long engagement, Alex and I were married in a private civil ceremony with only our closest friends and immediate family in attendance. This was followed by a larger outdoor party on the green lawn at his mother's home.

Since it was an outdoor party, I wore a cocktail length cream-colored dress, and Alex wore a light summer suit. He invited all his pals from the department, including the chief, and I invited a number of my coworkers from the hospital. His parents sprung for a tent and hired a band. All this was planned in three short weeks, and on that night, we danced until 2:00 in the morning.

Alex and I—now husband and wife—drove off in the Buick with a uniformed chauffeur and a "Just Married" sign taped to the back window. We spent the night at the Hilton in Hartford, and the next morning, flew to Niagara Falls for a three-day honeymoon in a luxurious suite with a heart-shaped hot tub.

It was the most romantic experience of my life and I'll remember it always, though it was to be short lived.

The following Wednesday morning, we were both back at work for morning shifts, and life in the real world resumed.

❧

The following spring, I gave birth to a beautiful baby girl who came into the world at eight pounds, eleven ounces. She was the most exquisite creature I'd ever seen—with her father's dark hair and compelling eyes. Her lips, nose and chin, however, definitely came from my side of the family.

Alex exceeded all my expectations as a husband and father. He changed diapers and was a great source of emotional support for me as I learned to breast-feed. At night when Wendy cried, he rose from bed to bring her to me without ever needing to be asked, and he rubbed my feet when I was tired. He also washed dishes and picked up groceries and doted on Wendy tirelessly with all the love a father could possibly give.

"You're going to spoil her," I said with a smile one evening as I joined him on the sofa where he was cradling our newborn in his arms.

"Probably," he replied, gently placing her soother in her mouth. "But when she's sixteen and the boys start coming around, I'll be waiting in the shadows with my fire hose."

I laughed. "The water pressure alone should send them down the stairs in a hurry. She won't like it."

Alex rubbed her sweet little head and spoke softly in front of her face. "Yes, you will, won't you? Because you won't have time for boys. You'll be too busy with schoolwork and ballet classes."

I chuckled again. "Ballet? What if she wants to play hockey?"

"That'll be all right," he replied. "She can be anything she wants to be." Then his eyes lifted and he regarded me with adoration. "We made a good baby."

"Yes, we certainly did."

"Want to make another one?" he asked with a flirty smile.

I laughed again. "Are you sure you're ready for that?"

"I'm ready whenever you are, gorgeous. All you have to do is say the word."

Inclining my head, I stood up and held out my hand. "That sounds like an offer I simply can't refuse."

Those were the happiest days of my life, when Alex and I were newlyweds. All my doubts and fears about his ability to be a good husband fell away, and I let myself fall. I loved him deeply and passionately with every inch of my soul, and had no regrets about rushing into this marriage.

At the time, I believed it was the best and bravest thing I'd ever done—to take that leap of faith and just *believe*.

Two months later I discovered I was pregnant again. I lost the baby, however, in a painful miscarriage that left me devastated—so much so, that my mother had to come and stay with us for two weeks to help take care of Wendy.

Alex was strong for the both of us, but I knew how disappointed he was, especially when we found out it was a boy.

"We're young," he said. "We'll have another. We'll have as many as we want."

The doctor assured us there was no permanent damage from the miscarriage. He told me I'd be able to conceive again as soon as we were ready.

I couldn't imagine ever being ready, though, because I was still so grief-stricken.

But I *tried* to imagine it. Every day I made a sincere effort, looked into my daughter's eyes and strove to see the future.

It was impossible, of course. There were no crystal balls. All I could do was thank God for the present and cherish the blessings I already had.

Not long after Wendy's second birthday, I began to notice subtle differences in Alex's behavior.

We'd been trying to have another baby for a while, but for some reason it hadn't happened and I was beginning to feel anxious. *What if the doctor was wrong? What if something bad happened to me when I miscarried? What if he missed something?*

Or maybe Alex and I were simply fated to have only one child. I hoped that wouldn't be the case because we both wanted a big family. Three children at least. Maybe four or five if we had the energy.

But here we were…month after month…unable to conceive.

"Just give it time," everyone said to me. "Don't worry. It will happen when it's meant to happen."

But I wanted it to happen *now*. I was tired of waiting.

And I was worried about Alex.

Distracted.

That's the word I would use to describe him in the weeks following Wendy's second birthday.

I asked him if I had done or said something wrong, but he assured me everything was fine. Nevertheless I felt a distance between us I'd never felt before, and it made me feel empty and lonely inside.

I wondered if it was me. I hadn't been myself since the miscarriage. I even began to wonder if I was depressed. Then I realized it had been ages since Alex and I had gone out on a proper date, laughed together, or made love. I certainly smiled less often—and of course being a mother to a busy two-year-old was exhausting. It had been a long time since I'd felt the least bit sexy.

I told myself this was normal for new parents. I also knew it wasn't just me. Alex seemed exhausted too. One night he looked particularly pale, so I asked if he'd been to see a doctor lately.

He told me not to worry; he wasn't sick. He was just busy at work.

I wouldn't have worried at all if he hadn't started coming home late most nights.

Whenever I asked what had kept him, he seemed caught off guard. Then he explained that he was taking an online course to upgrade his firefighter certification and didn't want to bring his work home with him.

Naturally I gave him the benefit of the doubt because I didn't want to be paranoid. I didn't want to go back to the uncertainties I'd felt when we were dating.

Later I would realize it was a mistake to have done so. I should have pressured him to tell me the truth. It would have saved me a lot of grief later on.

Twenty-four

Sometimes it seems remarkable how certain moments of our lives stand out from all the others with striking clarity, and are burned into our memories forever.

Take, for instance, the collapse of the twin towers. Most of us remember exactly where we were when we learned of it.

Sometimes it's a single moment from your childhood which is vivid and clear, while all the others fade into the blurred tapestry of our past.

There is one memory I have of my grandfather giving me a dime to go to the candy store down the street from where he and my grandmother lived. Whenever I recall the thrill of seeing that shiny coin drop into my small hand, it feels like something out of a dream. Other times it feels like it happened only yesterday. It had been more than a decade since we buried my grandfather. He was a kind and wonderful man.

The other memory that will never fade from my mind occurred on the day I received the life-changing phone call from David. I don't know how I managed to survive it. I suppose it was Wendy who helped me get through it all. Because of her, I had no choice but to stay strong.

The ring tone made me jump.

I'd been wandering down the breakfast aisle in the grocery store when I fumbled to answer my cell phone. "Hello?"

"Hi Audrey? It's Cathy. Are you watching the news?"

"No, I'm getting groceries," I replied. "Why? What's happening?"

I tossed a box of cereal into my cart and shifted the phone from one ear to the other. Wendy leaned over the side of the cart to reach for one of the sugary cereals in a colorful box, but I whispered, "Not that one," and helped her sit up straight again.

"A bomb went off in an office building downtown," Cathy explained.

I stopped in my tracks.

"All the Manchester engines are there," she continued, "and they think it might be a terrorist attack. They're not sure, though. It could also have been some idiot teenager."

"Oh God," I said. "Do you see Alex?"

"It's impossible to make anyone out," she replied. "All the firefighters are there in full gear, so he must be there. It looks really bad."

Suddenly needing to hear Alex's voice and know that he was okay, I squeezed my eyes shut. "I'm going to hang up and call him on his cell," I said. "He probably won't answer, but I have to try."

"Call me right back," she said.

My stomach churned as I speed-dialed his number, but I was put through to voice mail.

"Hi Alex, it's me. I heard about the bomb. Please call when you get a chance so I know you're okay."

I ended the call and took a few deep breaths, then hurried to the checkout and called Cathy back.

The rest of the day was its own version of hell. I tried to get downtown to the fire but all the streets had been closed off, so I drove to Cathy's house to watch the footage on television. The explosion made national headlines and a reporter from CNN was on the scene.

I searched for Alex among the chaos, but it was impossible to recognize any individual firefighter because they all wore bulky coats, helmets and face masks. A number of them were operating hoses from the parking lot, and it was reported that some had gone inside the burning building to look for survivors.

Please, God, keep him safe. I quietly prayed while Wendy toddled around Cathy's living room, oblivious to what was happening on television.

I watched with bated breath as one of the reporters interviewed witnesses and spoke to a woman who worked in the building. She'd gone out for a brief walk in the fresh air during her break when the bomb went off.

"You must be living under a shining star," the reporter said.

The woman burst into tears because there was still no word about her coworkers.

I, too, wanted to burst into tears, but I kept it together. "I wish he'd call me," I said to Cathy.

"He will," she replied. "I'm sure you'll hear something soon."

I was standing at Cathy's kitchen island when my cell phone rang in the back pocket of my jeans.

The vibration caused me to jump and I scrambled to reach my phone. Checking the call display, I was disappointed to see that it wasn't Alex. It was a number I didn't recognize.

Just then the news correspondent on television appeared on screen to report that a floor had just collapsed in the building, and they weren't sure yet if any firefighters had been in that location at the time.

"Hello?" I said.

"Audrey, is that you?"

I didn't recognize the man's voice. There was a lot of noise in the background. "Yes, it's me," I replied. "Who's this?"

"It's David," he said. "Where are you?"

"I'm at Cathy's house. What's going on?"

"Oh, God. It's bad. You better get down to the hospital right away. They just took Alex away in an ambulance."

My heart rate skyrocketed. "*What*? What happened? Is he all right?"

"I don't know," David replied. "He was in the building when the floor collapsed but they pulled him out. He's in bad shape, Audrey. He's unconscious."

"Oh, no…" I cupped my forehead in a hand. My gaze shot to Cathy who was sitting on the sofa with Wendy on her lap.

"What is it?" she asked.

I shook my head at her and finished talking to David. "Thanks for calling me. I'm heading to the hospital now. Be safe, okay?"

"I will," he replied.

We ended the call and I shoved the phone back into my pocket. "Can you watch Wendy? Alex was in the building when the floor collapsed. They just took him to the hospital."

"Of course," she replied with concern, standing up with Wendy in her arms. "Do you need me to go with you?"

"Not right now." I crossed the room to grab my jacket and purse. "I'm sure they'll be needing help at the hospital, so I might not be back for a while. I'll call as soon as I know something."

With that I kissed Wendy on the forehead and hurried out the door.

Twenty-five

❧

I arrived in the ER and I found Alex in the trauma room. He was lying on a backboard with a neck brace and had just been intubated.

"What's happening?" I asked. "What can I do?"

Dr. O'Brien shot me a look. "You should wait outside, Audrey."

I stared at him with stricken eyes. "No. I need to be here. Let me help."

"No way," he firmly said, then he paused, and his voice softened. "You can stay, but only if you stand back."

I quickly nodded and backed up against the door.

My heart had been pounding with absolute terror since I left Cathy's house. Now that I was here, I understood why Dr. O'Brien didn't want my help. As I watched him work quickly and skillfully on my husband, my stomach burned and I feared I might be sick.

"There's a large contusion at the left temple," Dr. O'Brien said, "and an open wound in the occipital area. There's some movement with the bone so it looks like an open skull fracture."

I covered my mouth with a hand to keep from crying out because I knew how serious that was, and I was afraid they'd force me to leave if I became hysterical.

I had thought, coming in here, that I could maintain my composure—I was well accustomed to urgent trauma cases—but this was very different. It was my husband on the table. My *husband*.

"Mr. Fitzgerald," Dr. O'Brien said, leaning over him. "Can you hear me? Can you open your eyes?"

Alex offered no response.

The doctor pressed on Alex's nail beds and used his knuckles to bear down on his sternum. Again there was no motor response, not even any show of posturing.

I watched as the team set up the portable X-ray machine and took pictures of Alex's chest, pelvis, legs and C-spine. Both his legs had been shattered, but thankfully there was no internal bleeding, nor any damage to his spine.

Dr. O'Brien addressed a nurse, Maureen, one of my closest friends in the ER. "We need to prep him for a CAT scan."

Just then, the clerk, Jeremy, pushed through the door. "We have three more traumas coming in, and we're going to need all the help we can get."

Dr. O'Brien turned to me. "Can you keep it together, Audrey? Can you go with Jeremy?"

"Yes, I'm fine, but why don't I take Alex to the CAT scan?"

"No," he replied. "Maureen will do that, but you can help with the other traumas if you're sure you're up for it."

I heard sirens wailing outside the ER and watched the team rush out of the room. "I'm sure, but I'll need to know what's going on with Alex. Will you promise to keep me informed?"

"I will."

I accepted his reply and forced myself to focus on the urgent cases that were about to land in the ER. Quickly I ran to change into a pair of scrubs.

One of the trauma cases turned out to be a coworker of Alex's named Jim who had been a guest at our wedding. He was the least serious case—brought in for smoke inhalation and a broken collarbone—and he was able to relay some details about what happened to Alex.

Jim said there were no flames in the area where Alex had been injured. He'd gone in looking for one of the other firefighters they'd lost contact with. Alex had found him in a restroom with a woman who was locked in a stall, petrified and refusing to come out.

That's when the ceiling collapsed on top of them. Alex had pushed the other firefighter out of the way when a steel girder came down. The woman was rescued, but they had to bring in the Jaws of Life to rescue Alex.

As far as Jim knew, Alex had been knocked unconscious and hadn't woken up, not even when they were pulling him out of the wreckage.

Though I maintained a professional focus for the next hour, in my mind I was screaming.

"Any news?" I asked Maureen when she returned to the floor.

"Not yet," she said, "but the radiologist is looking at the scans now."

My chest throbbed. The fact that Alex's legs were shattered meant a long, arduous road of treatment and recovery—but that was the *best* case scenario. *What if there was irreparable damage to his brain? What if he never woke up at all?*

A short while later, Dr. O'Brien found me in the supply room where I had gone to fetch some sterile coated sutures.

"Audrey, can I talk to you?" He shut the door, which caused my stomach to drop.

Somehow—I don't know how—I found the courage to face him squarely.

"We've looked at the scans," he told me, "and the news isn't good." He paused and looked down at the suture packages in my hands. "You probably shouldn't be working right now." He took them from me and set them back on the shelf. "We can handle things from here. You're going to need to focus on your family."

Taking a deep breath to smother the panic rising up inside me, I dropped my hands to my sides. "Why? Tell me the truth and please don't sugarcoat it. I need to know everything."

Though it was not easy to hear, I was thankful that he spoke frankly.

"I'm sorry to tell you this," he said, "but your husband has suffered a massive brain trauma. There's blood and clot everywhere, and it's going to be impossible for him to come back from damage that severe."

My hands began to shake, but I strove to keep my voice steady. "Surely there must be *some* hope? Is there not even the smallest chance that he could come out of it?"

Dr. O'Brien shook his head. "I'm sorry, there's none. His entire left hemisphere is pulverized. I can show you the scans if you like. His brain just isn't salvageable. He's not coming back."

It took a moment or two for the words to sink in, then my entire body turned to pulp and my knees buckled. I dropped to a sitting position on the floor and began to weep.

Dr. O'Brien knelt on one knee before me and laid a hand on my shoulder. "I'm so sorry. He was a good man." He gave me a moment to get over the shock and collect myself, then he reached for a box of tissues on the shelf beside us and opened it. He handed me one and I blew my nose. "I'm so sorry," he said again. "Is there anyone we should call?"

"I already called Alex's parents," I told him. "They were in Boston today but they're on their way here now."

I wiped the last few tears from my cheeks, then Dr. O'Brien offered a hand to help me rise.

"Thank you," I said. "You've been very kind."

He was quiet for a moment, then spoke gently. "I know it's hard to think about this right now, but outside of Alex's brain injury and his legs, his body is healthy and strong. He was a hero in this lifetime, Audrey—but he could still save more lives if you're willing to consider organ donation. I hope you'll think about it."

I nodded my head, but my mind had gone blank. I wasn't capable of making a decision like that—not now when I couldn't even fathom the idea of losing my husband, the man I loved...the father of my child.

I was in shock.

As I walked out of the supply room, all I could do was focus on finding a place to sit down before I collapsed again.

Two Years Later

Another Life…

Nadia Carmichael

I f there is one thing I believe in, it is the strength of the human heart.

My name is Nadia Carmichael and I am the grateful recipient of a gift from a man named Alex Fitzgerald—a man who died and gave his heart to a stranger.

Just over two years ago, when I was pregnant with my daughter, Ellen, I contracted a mysterious virus that attacked my heart muscle and sent me into cardiac failure.

To this day I am still amazed that my own heart managed to function long enough and well enough for me to give birth to my beautiful baby by C-section. And then, within a month I was lucky enough to receive word that a suitable donor heart had become available.

If not for that heart, and the miracle of modern medicine, I would not be alive today and my daughter would not have a mother.

Well…Someone would have stepped into that role—my twin sister, Diana, most likely—but it wouldn't have been me. I would never have known the joy of watching my baby take her first steps and utter her first words. And there was still so much to look forward to.

Nor would I be a married woman today, because my husband Jesse had come along many months after my transplant. We met when I was finally beginning to feel healthy again, like a normal person, believing there was hope that I had, at long last, come out the other side of that ordeal—even stronger than before.

But there is still more story to tell. A great deal more, in fact. And it all started with a dream.

There are many different kinds of dreams. Some occur when we sleep, when our minds create stories we can observe as if we were watching a movie. Others occur during the day when we are fully awake and in complete control of where our imagination takes us. Then there are dreams that are wishes—and those sorts of dreams can help us set goals and achieve great things.

I once dreamed I would meet Prince Charming, that he would arrive in a white stretch limo and rescue me from my minimum wage existence. I was seventeen at the time, but it proves to me that dreams do come true, because I *did* meet Prince Charming—though he came for me in a silver Volkswagen Jetta.

That was enough. It was quite perfect, actually. Or rather, *he* was perfect.

Jesse and I have been married just over a year now, and until he came along, I never imagined how good life could be.

Not long after my heart transplant, I began to have a recurring dream that I was flying. Usually I flew towards dark, starry skies, then coasted smoothly and quietly over cities, mountains, or fields.

I never felt afraid, and when I woke I was often in a relaxed and peaceful state.

Eventually I began to recognize the locations beneath me, and one night I realized I was flying over the transplant center—the very place where my life had begun anew.

Maybe I'm superstitious by nature, but I couldn't help but wonder if I was somehow connecting with the spirit of my donor. Was he flying through my window at night to check on his old heart? Did I somehow sense his presence in my dreams? Was he taking me places?

Then, about eight months after my transplant, I attempted to connect with his family by sending a letter of gratitude. I had to do this through the Donor Network, because personal identities of donors and recipients are kept confidential, unless both parties specifically and independently express a desire to meet.

When I finally sent my letter, this is the reply I received:

To the recipient of my son's heart,

Thank you for your letter. It meant a great deal to us to learn that something good came from my son's passing—that you are alive now because of the choice he made to donate his organs. We have heard from some others as well, so it appears his generosity has helped more than a few people.

Thank you again for telling us about your improved health. We were pleased and uplifted to hear it.

We wish you all the best.

Sincerely,

The Donor Family

Recognizing the family's desire to move on—and their lack of interest in meeting me—I did not try to contact them again, and instead focused on moving forward with my own life as well.

Except for one small moment of weakness…

After discovering my donor's obituary online—and learning about his career as a firefighter and the wife and child he left behind—I strapped Ellen into her car seat one day, got behind the wheel, and drove to Mr. Fitzgerald's home town.

All I wanted to do was see where he'd lived and worked, and walk the same sidewalks he had walked.

This adventure took me to the address where he'd resided in a third-floor flat, and to the public playground across the street where I unintentionally met his widow Audrey and his young daughter, Wendy.

Caught off guard when they joined Ellen and me in the playground, I chose not to reveal my identity.

Many months later, I would wish that I had, for I've learned it would have saved Audrey a great deal of grief and heartache.

When I returned home from our picnic in the Manchester playground, I vowed to finally put it all behind me. I *did* lay it to rest, and for a long time I was content to truly claim this new heart as my own.

But then I received another letter—and my interest in Alex Fitzgerald came alive again.

"I wanted to wait until you came home," I said to my husband Jesse when he walked through the door after work. "I couldn't bring myself to open it. I have a weird feeling about it."

The letter from the Donor Network had arrived earlier in the day and the first thing I did was call Jesse on his cell phone to tell him about it.

He shrugged out of his jacket and hung it on the coat tree. "Where is it?"

"On the table." I followed him into the kitchen where he picked up the envelope, turned it over and looked at it. "Do you want me to read it first?"

I considered that. "No. I think I should."

He nodded and handed it over.

I took a deep breath and broke the seal. "But stay here."

"Don't worry," he replied as he pulled out a chair to sit down. "I'm just as curious as you are."

I sat down across from him at the table and unfolded the letter. It was written by hand on tasteful stationery that looked as if it had been purchased at an expensive boutique. "The penmanship is the same as last time," I said.

"It must be his mother," Jesse replied, because I'd shown him the previous letter and we'd both agreed it looked like a woman's handwriting.

I read the letter with Jesse leaning over my shoulder.

To the recipient of my son's heart. I hope this letter finds you well. I can't believe it's been two years since my son passed. We still miss him every day.

My gaze lifted. I turned my head and shared a look with Jesse, because neither of us could imagine how it would feel to lose a child.

I lowered my gaze and continued reading.

I want to thank you again for writing to us after your transplant. I was pleased and comforted to learn that you were doing well and seemed so happy. I am writing to you now because lately I find myself wondering about you. I hope you are still doing well and that my son's heart is continuing to provide you with that "second chance at life" you mentioned before. If you are inclined to write to me again, I would enjoy hearing from you.
Sincerely,
Your donor's mom.

I folded the letter and looked up.

"Wow," Jesse said. "That's different from last time. She's definitely reaching out."

"Maybe she just needed time to grieve," I replied. "It was probably too soon before. It was too much to handle."

Jesse nodded. "Now that some time has passed, I can under-stand how she'd want to know how you're doing. You do have her son's heart. Are you going to write back?"

I slipped the letter into the envelope. "Of course. I want her to know I'm okay. Better than okay. I'll write to her tonight."

—⤸

It was tempting to open my letter with "Dear Mrs. Fitzgerald," but I wasn't supposed to know her identity, or Alex's for that mat-ter—I had discovered that quite on my own last year. But even so, I had no idea if this woman was even a "Mrs. Fitzgerald." Perhaps she had remarried and was now a Mrs. Smith or Jones. So I adhered to the Donor Network's code of confidentiality, and this is what I wrote:

To the mother of my heart donor,

Thank you so much for writing to me. I was touched by your letter and I am happy to report that I'm still doing won-derfully well. Your son's heart is working like a charm for me and my health is better than ever. I exercise regularly and go for gorgeous nature hikes with my husband and daughter, and I am taking very good care of myself, eating well and never taking for granted the strong heart inside of me.

My daughter just turned two and she's very bright. She keeps me busy. Since the last time I wrote to you, my hus-band and I bought a beautiful house on the water, so we are enjoying the task of completing some household projects, as it was an older home and required some updating.

This whole experience of getting sick and finding my way back to health has taught me many things about the importance of treasuring each day and appreciating our loved ones. I have your son to thank for giving me the opportunity to learn these precious life lessons, which I will never forget.

    At the same time, I still mourn for your loss. Having a child of my own, I can only imagine how difficult it must have been for you. I don't know much about your son, but I do know he had a great heart.

    Sincerely...

Oh, how I wanted to sign my own name, but I knew that I couldn't. If I did, the Donor Network wouldn't allow it. I didn't know what they would do. Would they even deliver it?

    Instead, I signed the letter, "A Friend," but indicated in writing in a separate cover letter to the administrators at the Network that if the family ever wanted to meet me, I would be happy to oblige.

    Three weeks later, I received a phone call that blew my mind.

❝Hello?" I struggled to balance the phone between my ear and shoulder because I was trying to buckle Ellen into her booster seat at the table. She wasn't in the mood to cooperate, however, because she wanted to be tickled.

"Hi Nadia, it's Marg from the Donor Network. How are you doing today?"

I felt a rush of nervous butterflies in my stomach. "I'm great," I replied, snapping the buckle on Ellen's seat and placing the bowl of cereal in front of her. "It's nice to hear from you."

After making sure that Ellen was settled and digging into her breakfast, I moved away from the table so I wouldn't be distracted.

"We got your letter about wanting to meet your donor's family," Marg said, "and I sent your note on to them, letting them know that it could be arranged if they were interested. Today I got an email from your donor's mother and she's wondering if you'd like to set up a time to meet. If you like, I can give you some information about the family and you can take the time you need to make up your mind."

My breath hitched in my throat. *They wanted to meet me?* I was both overjoyed and intimidated, because I was using their son's heart and benefiting greatly from it, while they had lost him forever. I know it wasn't my fault he had died, but there was still a part of me that felt incredibly guilty about that.

I fought to sweep all those doubts and insecurities from my mind, however, and quickly answered the question.

"I'd love to know more about them," I said to Marg. "What can you tell me?"

"I'll start with their names," she said. "First of all, your donor. His name was Alex Fitzgerald and he didn't live that far from you, in Manchester, Connecticut. He was a firefighter."

I swallowed over a spark of excitement that rose up within me upon hearing his name—even though I already knew it.

"I see," I replied, not letting Marg know I'd already known this.

"His mother's name is Jean and she's married to Garry Martel, who was Alex's stepfather. His real father passed away when he was very young. He also has a younger sister named Sarah who is in her early twenties and works in Boston. Jean and Garry live in Manchester, and in Jean's email she suggested that you and she could meet for lunch anywhere that's convenient for you. I didn't tell her where you lived because I didn't have your permission to do that, but whatever you want to share, I can pass that along and put the two of you in touch directly."

"That would be great," I said. "Please, when you reply to her email, tell her my name and that I live in Waltham. I'd be happy to come to Manchester, or if she'd prefer to meet somewhere neutral, like in Boston, that would be okay, too. Tell her my husband's name is Jesse Fraser and he's a helicopter pilot, and our daughter's name is Ellen and she's two years old. And you can give her my full address, phone number and email. I'll wait for her to contact me."

"Great," Marg said. "I've got all this and I'll send her an email right now. Good luck, Nadia, and if you wouldn't mind keeping me posted about what happens..."

"I will. Thank you, Marg."

We hung up, and I turned around to face Ellen who was just finishing her cereal.

"Want some more?" I asked.

Ellen nodded her head, so I grabbed the box and poured, realizing only then that Marg hadn't mentioned anything about Alex's wife or child. Audrey's name hadn't even come up.

CHAPTER

Twenty-nine

❦

Twenty minutes after I spoke to Marg, my phone rang again. This time the call display said Garry Martel, so there was no question who it was—the mother of my organ donor.

For two years, I had been living a new and beautiful life with her son's heart beating inside of my chest, and I'd wanted desperately to meet her in person, to embrace her and convey the affection I felt for her.

Intellectually I knew it was silly to feel so connected to a woman who was, effectively, a complete stranger to me. We weren't related, yet I had her DNA inside of me.

The whole thing was totally bizarre and my heart was beating like a drum when I picked up the phone.

"Hello?" I said tentatively.

"Hi, may I speak with Nadia Fraser?" She sounded formal but friendly.

"This is Nadia," I replied.

There was a brief, momentary pause. "Hi, Nadia," she finally said. "This is Jean Martel. The Organ Donor Network gave me your number."

"Yes," I quickly replied. "It's so nice to hear from you."

There was another excruciatingly long pause.

"This is strange, isn't it?" she said with laughter in her voice, and my whole body relaxed. I was worried it might be an emotional phone call and there would be weeping, but she sounded at ease with the situation.

"It sure is," I replied. "But I'm really glad you called. I've wanted to meet you for such a long time because I feel so incredibly connected to you." I stopped myself. "Oh, gosh. That must have sounded crazy. I'm sorry. I'm actually a very levelheaded person."

"Don't apologize," she said. "I've had the same thoughts. For me, it feels like a part of my son is still alive out there in the world because of what he gave. And you were always the recipient I wondered about the most because you were the one who got his heart. Maybe it's sentimental of me, but something feels special about that."

I smiled. "It feels special to me, too."

I chose not to bring up the subject of my flying dreams, or the fact that I believed her son's spirit had helped me through a very difficult experience a year ago when I contracted pneumonia and was rushed to the hospital. Instead, I focused on the here and now.

"Marg told me you live in Manchester," I said. "We're not that far from each other. I live in Waltham."

"Yes, Marg mentioned that," Jean said, "and I would love to get together with you in person if you're interested. I was thinking we could meet for lunch somewhere, but now that we've had a chance to speak, I feel more comfortable asking if you'd like to come and visit us at our home. I'm sure you're as curious about Alex as we are about you. I could show you some photo albums and tell you more about his life. I think I'm ready for that now. I wasn't before."

My heart leapt. To learn more about my donor was a dream come true.

"I understand," I replied, "and I would love to come and visit you. When would be a good time?"

We talked it over and made arrangements for Saturday afternoon. She gave me her address and told me to bring Jesse and Ellen.

I hung up and felt a great swell of joy move through me. I scooped Ellen into my arms and hugged her tight.

"On Saturday we're going to meet a very nice lady," I said. "She's not exactly your grandmother," I added, "but she sort of is, in a weird sort of way."

Then something struck me, and my stomach clenched tight.

What if Audrey was there? Surely she'd remember me from the day we met in the playground across the street from her house. She'd wonder why I didn't tell her who I was.

How would I explain that I knew where she lived because I'd met her husband in a dream?

I hoped she wouldn't think I'd been stalking her.

"Wow, nice place," Jesse said as we pulled up in front of the Martel's home.

"Gorgeous," I replied. "I just hope this doesn't turn out to be awkward." I was referring to Audrey being there.

"It'll be fine," he said. "If you tell them about your dreams, they'll understand why you needed to know more, and the fact that you didn't break the rules about confidentiality says a lot about you, because you could have contacted them outside of the Donor Network, but you didn't. You respected their privacy."

We got out of the car and I opened the back door to unbuckle Ellen from her car seat. "I just hope *they* see it that way."

"I'm sure they will, as long as you're upfront about it."

I set Ellen down on the pavement and held her hand as we entered the driveway, which was beautifully landscaped with lush green shrubs, tall cedars and a stone walkway that led to the front door.

My heart beat thunderously in my ears as we stepped onto the flagstone veranda and Jesse reached for the doorbell.

"I can't believe we're finally here," I said, "and I'm going to see the house where he lived."

Jesse massaged the back of my neck. "It's a big day."

Ellen reached her hands out to Jesse. He picked her up and held her in his arms while we waited for someone to answer the door.

Footsteps approached from inside, and the door swung open.

For a moment I couldn't breathe as I found myself staring at the woman who must be Jean, Alex Fitzgerald's mother. She was exactly as I imagined her to be—warm and friendly and outwardly classy. Her gray hair was swept into a loose bun on top of her head, and her floral printed dress was both casual and cheerful.

"You must be Nadia," she said with a smile. A man appeared behind her to greet us as well. I assumed he was her husband, Alex's stepfather.

"Come in," she said, opening the door wider and inviting us inside. "I'm Jean and this is Garry."

Jesse introduced himself and Ellen, and we all shook hands.

"We're so glad you could come," Jean said.

I held out the bottle of white wine we'd brought with us. "This is for you."

"How lovely," she replied, taking the bottle from my hands. "Shall we open it now? Or can we get you something else? A cocktail or iced tea?"

"I'd love some iced tea," I said as we all moved into the large kitchen.

I looked out the back windows at a charming stone patio with a table and chairs made of teak, surrounded by greenery. Wildflowers and a selection of colored glass ornaments turned the space into something resembling a magical fairy land.

There was something so familiar about all of this, and I wondered if I imagined that. "What a lovely home you have," I said.

"Thank you," Jean replied. "We've been very happy here."

So far it was just the five of us, and though I wanted to meet Alex's sister and other members of his family, for the time being I was relieved. This would at least give me a chance to talk to Jean and Garry about the dreams I'd had, and explain how I already knew their son's identity…long before she had called.

⁓

Eventually we moved outside to the patio and sat down to enjoy our drinks and nibble on crackers, sliced cheese and grapes—all displayed attractively on a shiny silver platter.

Ellen was rambunctious as usual, but Jean was patient and kind. She held Ellen on her lap and let her play with her keys and cell phone.

Later Jesse suggested he take Ellen for a walk around the yard. This left me alone with Jean and Garry, and the conversation turned to deeper matters.

"Did you feel different when you woke up from the surgery?" Garry asked. "I've often wondered about that—if having someone else's heart inside you might introduce new thoughts or feelings. Or maybe that's a silly question."

"It's not silly at all," I replied. "Some transplant patients have reported things like hating certain foods or activities before, then discovering they loved them afterward. As far as I know, there's no real scientific proof to support these things. It's just one of those unexplained mysteries of modern medicine."

"Did you have any changes in tastes for food or activities?" he asked. "If you did, maybe we could verify whether or not it had anything to do with Alex."

"What was his favorite food?" I asked.

Jean smiled. "He loved mushrooms fried in butter and served with a steak."

"Mmm," I replied. "I love that, too, but I loved it before the transplant, so we can't blame Alex."

They smiled and nodded, and I felt very at home with them. They were nice people.

"I've had some strange dreams, though," I added, deciding it was a good opportunity to bring them up.

"What kinds of dreams?" Garry asked, sitting forward in his chair.

I inclined my head slightly. "This is going to sound a bit strange."

Jean reached across the table and covered my hand with hers. "You can tell us."

My heart warmed at the sensation of her touch.

"Well…" I began to explain. "Not long after the surgery, I starting having a recurring dream that I was flying. It's not an uncommon dream. Lots of people have it, so I looked it up. Most dream interpreters say that as long as you're flying without fear and you feel you are in control, it means you overcame some sort of challenge in your life and you feel empowered."

"That makes sense in your case," Jean said. "After what you went through…"

I nodded. "Yes, absolutely, but there was a bit more to it than that. Sometimes I dreamed I was flying over the hospital where I had my surgery, and I started to wonder if maybe I was remembering or reliving some kind of out-of-body experience." I paused. "Am I getting too crazy? Is this too much?"

"No, I'm riveted," Jean replied. "I read a book recently about a woman who drowned in a frozen lake, but they were able to bring her back after forty minutes because her body was so cold.

She claims to have had a near-death experience and says she interacted with family members who were already dead."

"Is that *The Color of Heaven*?" I asked. "I read that book, too, and I met the author."

"Did you really? What was she like?"

"Very down to earth," I replied. "I talked to her about my dreams and she was very helpful."

Jean sat back and stared at me intently. "Tell me more about the dreams. Did you see Alex in them?"

I took a moment to collect my thoughts, because it wasn't an easy thing to tell a mother that yes, I did see her deceased son in a dream, and he told me his name.

Eventually, I nodded. "I think so. It happened a year ago when I was sick with pneumonia. I called an ambulance and lost consciousness on the way to the hospital. While I was out, I had another flying dream, but this time there was someone with me. He knew how afraid I was and he helped me stay calm. It wasn't until later, after I recovered, that I remembered the dream and the fact that he told me his name."

"What did he say?" Jean asked.

"He said his name was Alex."

She covered her mouth with a hand.

"As soon as I remembered that, I began to wonder if he was my donor, so I looked up some obituaries on line and found information about a firefighter named Alexander Fitzgerald who died on the same day I got my new heart. I just knew it was him."

Jean stared at me with fascination. "So you've known who he was for a while now."

I nodded. "Yes, but I couldn't contact you because of the confidentiality agreement. I'm not even sure I should have told you now. Maybe I shouldn't have."

Jean bowed her head and began to weep. Garry wrapped an arm around her.

"I'm very sorry," I softly said.

"It's fine," Garry replied. "We're glad you told us. It's both wonderful and difficult to hear."

My blood coursed quickly through my veins. I wanted to smother myself with a pillow for making Jean cry.

Her watery gaze lifted. "I've had my own dreams, too," she said, "though I'm never flying. And they're usually daydreams."

"What happens in them?" I asked.

She collected herself and sat back in the chair. "I'm usually here in the house and I swear I can hear him puttering about in the garage. Sometimes I think I hear him calling me, as if he wants me to bring him a drink of water or something."

"From the garage?" I asked.

She smiled and wiped her cheeks. "He loved working on his father's old car. Spent a lot of hours out there. The car's still there, beautifully restored. He used to say he wanted to pass it on to his firstborn, so we've been keeping it for our granddaughter, Wendy. When she's old enough, we'll give her the keys and papers. It'll be worth a lot of money by then."

"What kind of car is it?" I asked.

"It's a 1948 Buick Street Rod," Garry proudly replied. "Would you like to see it?"

"I'd love to."

Jesse and Ellen returned just then, and I stood up, eager to see the place where Alex had spent so much of his time, and see the car that had been so important to him.

"It's beautiful." I ran my hand over the shiny black hood of the car. "He did all this work himself?"

"That's right," Jean replied. "After his father died, I put it in storage for a number of years and eventually, when he got older, Alex started asking about it. He said he had fond memories of his father taking him to the race track. I'm amazed he'd remember that. He would have been very young."

"How old was he when your husband died?" I asked.

"He was nine."

"I'm so sorry," I said, and Jean nodded.

Jesse followed me deeper into the garage while keeping a close eye on Ellen.

"Are these his tools?" I asked, moving toward the work bench. I picked up a heavy wrench and held it in my hand, imagining Alex's hand gripping the same handle. Then I turned to face the car and could just see him lying on his back, his jean-clad legs sticking out from the undercarriage as he adjusted something.

Sometimes it felt like time passed in layers…that if I could hop down to another level in my mind, I could see him and talk to him.

What would I say?

I'd say thank you, of course.

"Do you come out here very often?" I asked Jean.

She shook her head. "Not so much lately. I used to, though. In the early weeks after he passed, I'd come just to sit in the car and cry." She paused. "He was such a good son."

Together we walked out of the garage to where the sun was shining brightly.

"How is your daughter doing?" I asked. "Marg mentioned her name was Sarah?"

"She's doing well. She works for a marketing firm in Boston and designs websites."

"That sounds like a fun job." I then treaded carefully around the next question. "And what about your daughter-in-law, Alex's widow? How is she holding up?"

Jean's shoulders rose and fell with a sigh. She looked away toward a tall row of cedars blowing in the wind. "Audrey took it pretty hard when we lost Alex, and she's still struggling. It's not easy at the best of times to be a single mom, and on top of that she's a nurse and has to do shiftwork. We take care of Wendy as much as we can, but sometimes I worry that Audrey will never be ready to move on."

"How do you mean?" I asked.

Jean met my gaze. "I hope she'll let herself love again some-day. I sincerely want that for her. The last time she was here—it was three weeks ago, the two-year anniversary of Alex's death—she went out to the garage and sat in that bloody car for over an hour. Then she left abruptly, barely saying good-bye to us. I just don't want to see her waste all the years of her life by not letting go of the past."

We began walking around the back of the house to the patio where Garry had lit the barbeque. The smell of steaks cooking on the grill caused my mouth to water. "Maybe she just needs a bit more time," I gently suggested.

"Maybe," Jean said, not sounding terribly optimistic. "I invited her to come today but she told me she couldn't bear to meet the woman who had Alex's heart beating inside of her."

I stopped on the lawn and looked up at the windows of the house. "I can sort of understand that."

I imagined if it was Jesse who had died and given his heart to another person—especially a woman—I'd feel slightly territorial, because Jesse's heart belonged to *me*.

But despite that, I'd still want him to be a donor—because I, of all people, knew the importance of organ donation.

Either way, it would still be difficult to face someone with his heart after I'd lost him.

Jean stopped as well. "Are you all right?" she asked. "You look troubled."

I dropped my gaze to the grass and began walking again. "I am a little, because I have something I need to confess to you."

Jean linked her arm through mine. "I'm sure it's nothing so terrible."

"It probably depends on who you're asking," I replied. "Remember when I told you that I looked up information about Alex after I had that dream?"

Jean nodded.

"Not long afterward, I couldn't help myself. I wanted to see where he lived and worked, so I drove here with Ellen. We found his apartment and stopped for a little while to play in the park across the street."

"The playground with the red slide?" Jean asked.

"Yes. And while we were there, your granddaughter saw us out her front window, and she and Audrey came outside to join us."

Jean's head drew back slightly. "Really. So you've already met Audrey? She never mentioned it."

"That's because I didn't tell her who I was," I admitted. "We had a nice time chatting, but she thought I was some random stranger. When I came here today, I was worried she'd be here and might be upset when she recognized me."

"Oh, my goodness," Jean replied. "That's quite a story. It must have been a shock when she walked out of the house."

"It was," I replied, "but I was glad I got to meet her. I loved how she talked about Alex. She said he had a good heart. It was a special moment I'll never forget."

We stepped onto the stone patio and Jean kissed Garry on the cheek. Turning to me as she opened the door to go inside, she said, "Help me set the table?"

I nodded and strode toward her.

"After we eat," she said, "I'll get out those photo albums I promised to show you."

"I can't wait to see them," I replied.

Jesse and Ellen came running across the lawn just then. Ellen was wearing a crown of daisies around her head.

"What have you been up to?" I cheerfully asked, lifting her up over my head.

"Playing," she replied, and I squeezed her against me.

The day had been quite perfect so far, and I was glad we had come. It hadn't been awkward at all.

At least not until later, when it was time to go.

After we said good-bye to Jean and Garry at the door, Jesse and I walked back to the car with Ellen between us holding both our hands.

"Elevator!" she said, wanting to play the game where Jesse lifted her up and down.

We both laughed and swung her like a little monkey between us.

When we reached the car, Jesse got into the driver's seat while I buckled Ellen into the back. As I was bent over, fiddling with the straps, I became vaguely aware of a car pulling up behind us and parking at the curb.

With Ellen fastened securely into her seat, I straightened and shut the door, then found myself standing face-to-face with a woman. For a few seconds I stared at her questioningly, then realized it was Audrey.

She glanced down at Ellen in the car seat, then back at me. "You…" she said.

My stomach did a somersault. "Yes," I replied. "I'm sorry, this is awkward."

"I'll say it is." Her cheeks flushed the color of two red hothouse tomatoes, and her chest heaved, as if she were suddenly hyperventilating. "What are you doing here?"

"I came to meet Jean and Garry," I replied. "They invited me."

Her eyebrows pulled together in a frown. She looked fit to be tied. "They *did*? My God."

Suddenly I realized I was not looking at a woman in pain who was still dealing with her grief. This was something else entirely. It was flat-out rage, and for the life of me, I couldn't understand why.

Seeing Through the Smoke

Audrey
Three Weeks Earlier

It had been two years since I was forced to watch Alex take his last breath. Or rather, I watched the machine do it for him. Wendy still had some memory of her father—mostly because I made a point to talk about him every day—but I worried that later in life, she would have trouble recalling anything about him.

Memories of early childhood are muddy at best for most of us. I certainly couldn't remember *anything* from my toddler years, though it helped to see pictures. I only wish I had used my camera more often during my brief marriage to Alex.

At least I'd had all of them printed at the local photography store. My collection of photos consisted of a somewhat archaic shelf of albums with cellophane-covered pages.

Who even has these anymore? I wondered as I stood in my living room one morning, staring at them. Everything in our modern world had gone digital in such a short span of time. Whenever I visited my friend's houses, all they had was a single battery-operated picture frame sitting on a shelf with a continuous dissolving slideshow.

I had to ask myself…what would happen if there was some sort of apocalypse, zombie or otherwise, where batteries were hard to come by? In a situation like that, only the photos printed on paper would be any good to look at. So I printed everything.

I needed our memories to survive, to never fade. I needed physical evidence of Alex's existence. Nothing less would do.

But it was that very physical evidence that nearly destroyed me on the second anniversary of his death. A part of me wishes I'd never unearthed that picture because the heartache that resulted was unimaginable.

Then I began to wonder if I was *meant* to unearth it…if Alex had somehow led me to it. Perhaps he had called to me from the great beyond. Jean sometimes said she felt as if he was still nearby, calling to her from the garage.

And so, I went there. I sat in the front seat of the old Buick that held so many special memories for us.

Then, in an instant, my life was turned upside down. Everything I believed in was crushed.

I was crushed, and I felt like a fool.

W hat was I looking for when I opened the glove box? Nothing. I was just bored and tired of weeping like a baby from behind the wheel, staring out the open garage doors at the row of cedars on the far side of the paved driveway.

You have to get over this, I told myself. *It's time to move on.*

But I couldn't. I simply couldn't let go. I could feel Alex, always at my side, whispering in my ear, telling me not to forget.

Though I loved him deeply, still, there were times when I resented him—or rather his ghost, if such a thing existed— for such selfishness. Why did he want to torture me like this? Wouldn't he prefer for my heart to heal? For me to find happiness again? To let go of the sadness and anger over the fact that he was taken from me, and I didn't even get to say good-bye?

Which brings me back to the moment I reached across the seat to open the glove box and rifle around inside.

What was in there?

Not much—just some old napkins from the time we went to a midnight drive-through on the way home from the movies, not long before Alex died. I had been working nights that week and was craving a burger with extra pickles. He got it for me, of course. He always said he wanted to give me everything.

He gave me Wendy, but he also caused me great pain from beyond the grave when that glove box door fell open.

⤳

Imagine my surprise when I discovered a picture of a baby which was taken during an ultrasound. At first glance I thought it must be Wendy, but as I peered closer I realized it was different from the picture I had of her.

Turning it over in my hand, I found a few words scribbled on the back in blue pen.

For Alex – I hope she has your good looks!
– C.

A tiny heart was drawn in the bottom right-hand corner and just below that, it was dated one week before Alex died.

I swallowed uneasily and tried to make sense of it. Were there any close family members who might have been expecting a child at that time—a cousin or a niece? His sister, Sarah, had never been pregnant, as far as I knew. And this note was signed with the initial "C."

For a long time I sat there, confused as I stared at the photo. Suddenly there was a ringing in my ears. Then I found myself fighting a wave of nausea that rose up in my belly as I recalled the weeks before Alex's death, when he came home late from work and seemed distracted all the time.

I wasn't proud of what I suspected while sitting in the front seat of his car—that he might have been having an affair— because he wasn't here to defend himself, and I certainly didn't want to become a jealous wife two years after his death, but what else could this be? My father always said, "If it looks like a duck and quacks like a duck, it's a duck."

Oh God…

My heart throbbed in the most excruciating way, and I closed my eyes. *Please, not this. Don't let it be this. Not my Alex.*

Tears filled my eyes and I couldn't seem to breathe without my ribs quaking and shuddering. How could this be?

No…it *couldn't* be.

For a long time I sat there in shock, overcome by a wave of grief that felt the same as it had when the doctor told me Alex's head injury was so severe, he would never open his eyes again. I don't think there is a way to describe the hurt I felt, knowing my worst fears had come true—that I had been wrong to trust my husband, and the love I believed to be special and mutual was not the forever kind—at least not for him.

I cried and cried until I was completely spent, then I slipped the photograph into the pocket of my jean skirt, got out of the car and went to collect Wendy. I had to say good-bye to Jean and Garry quickly before I lost control of my emotions again.

As soon as I arrived home, I pressed play on a DVD for Wendy and went a little crazy in my bedroom.

Not long after the first anniversary of Alex's death, I had cleaned out the closets and gotten rid of most of his personal belongings—a horrendous chore I didn't feel ready for at the time, but Cathy had encouraged me to do it.

Now there was little left to search through—no pockets where I might find evidence of a hotel room stay or a receipt for lingerie he never gave to me.

These were all terrible clichés, of course, which was why I felt completely delusional as I plugged in his old cell phone—one thing I had kept—and searched through all the calls from those final weeks. I found nothing out of the ordinary, no numbers I didn't recognize, no unfamiliar contact names that began with the letter C.

Tossing the phone onto the bed, I paced back and forth, not knowing what to do. I wished I was one of those women who could turn a blind eye and ignore unpleasant things. Why couldn't I just stuff the ultrasound photo into a trash bin on the street and sweep it from my mind?

Alex had been gone for two years now. I couldn't confront him or walk out on him in a huff. It would never lead to a divorce.

What was the point in even knowing the truth—if in fact there was something to know?

All that being said, I knew I'd never be able to let it go because I was *not* one of those women who could turn a blind eye, and I didn't want this photo to destroy the wonderful memories I had of my husband.

Besides, what if Alex had another child out there somewhere? A half-sister for Wendy? Didn't we both deserve to know the truth?

Surely someone had the answer. *But who?*

Sitting down on the bed, I stared at the telephone for a long moment and could think of only one person.

Alex's friend David had been a pallbearer at the funeral, and he had come around to the apartment a few times to lend a hand after Alex passed. He helped me set up a new computer when my old laptop was too slow, which I greatly appreciated because I was slightly tech-challenged.

He also took care of some practical details at the department, like making sure I received Alex's final paychecks and benefits and dealing with Alex's personal belongings in his locker.

Around that time, David started dating a female police officer and the last I'd heard, they'd moved in together. That was a year ago and I hadn't spoken to him in a long time, but now I had a good excuse to call.

Or maybe it wasn't exactly a *good* excuse. I didn't want David to think I was losing my mind, creating dramas just to keep Alex alive in my imagination.

But I had to find out the truth.

Since I didn't know David's number off hand, I reached for Alex's cell phone and found him in the list of contacts. Then I called from the landline on the bedside table.

David answered after the first ring. "Hello?"

The beat of my pulse accelerated. "Hi David. It's Audrey Fitzgerald."

"Hey," he gently replied. "It's great to hear from you. God, it's been way too long." He paused. "I'm sorry. That's my fault. I should have called to check on you. How are you doing?"

"No need to apologize," I said. "I'm doing well. Wendy's growing like a weed. She'll be starting school soon."

"Wow," he said. "That's great. Time sure flies. Are you still working in the ER?"

"Yes, as many shifts as I can get," I told him. "How about you? Are you still with the department?"

"Yep. Can't seem to imagine doing anything different."

There was an awkward pause, and I felt a sudden impulse to shovel words into it. "You're probably wondering why I'm calling."

"Kind of," he replied. "Not that it matters. I'm just glad to hear from you."

I sighed. "That's nice of you to say, David. Thank you, but now I feel really dumb. You're going think I'm crazy, and I probably am."

"What is it?" he asked, sounding both curious and concerned.

I didn't know where to begin. I didn't want to lead with the worst case scenario, so I attempted to ease into it.

"I've been thinking a lot about the last few weeks before Alex died. He had said he was taking some online courses to upgrade his certification. Do you know anything about that?"

David was quiet for a moment. "No, he never mentioned it to me. At least I don't remember anything. It was a long time ago."

I couldn't help but wonder if David knew something and was trying to protect Alex. Or maybe, with Alex gone, he was trying to protect *me*.

"Did you notice that he was staying late at work most nights?" I asked. "He told me he was working on the computer there."

For what seemed like a long while, David didn't say anything, and when he finally spoke his voice was husky and low. "Why are you asking me this, Audrey? Is there something going on?"

Hearing the added concern in his voice, I cupped my forehead in a hand and shut my eyes. Then I decided there was no point beating around the bush. If I wanted David to tell me what he knew, I was going to have to tell him what *I* knew.

"I found a picture in the Buick," I said. "It was an ultrasound of a baby in someone's womb—incidentally, not *my* womb—and there was a note written on the back. It said 'For Alex, I hope she gets your good looks.' It was signed with the initial C and dated a week before Alex died. There was a little heart drawn in the bottom corner."

"Do you still have the picture?" David asked.

"Yes, and I'm trying to figure out what it means. I don't want to assume the worst, but it's kind of hard not to because in those last few weeks, I did notice Alex seemed distracted." I paused. "Please, David, if you know something, will you tell me? I need to know the truth."

I flopped onto my back on the bed and braced myself for his reply.

"Honestly, I don't know anything," he told me. "Alex never confided in me about any secret affairs, if that's what you're thinking. And I can't imagine he would have cheated on you. He loved you and Wendy."

"Then why was this picture in the Buick?" I asked. "And why do I have this terrible gut feeling that he was hiding something?"

David thought about it. "I don't know. I wish I could offer you some insight, but I didn't notice anything unusual about him in those final weeks. He seemed fine to me."

I breathed a heavy sigh. "You must think I'm crazy, calling you like this."

"No, I don't," he said. "To be honest, I'd like to see the picture for myself."

"Why?"

"I'd like to take a look at the handwriting. Maybe it'll help me think of something. Are you doing anything right now?"

"No, I'm just sitting here, brooding."

He chuckled. "How about I come over? I've got nothing else to do."

"That would be great," I replied. "I'll see you in a few minutes."

I hung up and went to check on Wendy.

The first thing David did when he walked in the door was give me a hug. "It's good to see you," he said, then he glanced over at Wendy who was lying on the sofa, immersed in her movie. David approached her. "Hey kiddo, remember me?"

She looked up and smiled shyly, then nodded her head.

"What are you watching?" he asked.

"*Monsters, Inc.*"

He turned toward the television. "Yeah, I've seen this."

"The little girl isn't even scared."

David nodded. "You're right. She's pretty brave." He watched for another minute or two, then followed me into the kitchen.

"Want some coffee?" I asked.

"Sure."

I filled the coffee maker, pressed the start button and went to the cupboard to fetch two mugs. David leaned against the counter, watching me the whole time.

"So where is it?" he casually asked.

Knowing he was referring to the ultrasound picture, I picked it up off the pile of bills by the telephone and handed it to him.

He examined it, then flipped it over. When he read the note, his brow furrowed with displeasure. "This is strange," he admitted, "but it doesn't ring any bells. I'm sorry." He handed it back to me.

The coffeepot gurgled and I set the picture down on the counter.

"Tell me what you're thinking," David said. "You mentioned Alex was distracted those last few weeks."

"Yes, and he was coming home late. He said he was at the station working on that course. I was hoping you'd remember that."

David shook his head.

I opened the refrigerator door to get the milk. "Would the chief remember anything?" I asked. "Would he be able to tell me if David was enrolled in a course? I just want to know if he was telling me the truth about that."

"I can ask him," David replied. "But do you still have Alex's old cell phone? Have you checked that?"

"I did, and I didn't find anything."

"What about your old computer?" he asked. "Did you ever get rid of it?"

I had to think for a minute. "No, I still have it. I didn't want to trash it because all our personal information was on there. I can't believe I didn't think of that."

"Can you get it?" David asked. "I could check the history and see if he had any extra email accounts you might not have known about. Do you know his Facebook password?"

"Yeah, I do." Then I met David's gaze. "But I feel guilty about this—prying into Alex's personal life without his permission. It feels wrong and disrespectful."

I poured two cups of coffee and handed one to David.

"Don't feel guilty," he said. "You need peace of mind and you need to know where that picture came from. Even *I'll* admit to being curious. If I were in your shoes, I'd want to know."

I felt my shoulders relax slightly and set my coffee cup down on the table. "Wait here. I know where the old computer is. I'll go get it."

—⁓

By the time we had the old laptop plugged in and fired up at the kitchen table, the credits on the movie started to roll. Wendy jumped up off the sofa and turned off the television. "Can we go outside now?" she asked, running to wrap her arms around my legs.

I turned to David, who was already clicking buttons on the keyboard. "We have a firm rule in this house," I said. "Whenever credits roll on a movie—"

"We turn it off and go outside," Wendy finished for me.

"Unless it's bed time," I said to her. "Then what do we do?"

"Turn it off and go to bed!"

"That's right."

David's eyes lifted and he smiled at Wendy. "That's a good rule. You're mom's a very smart lady." He looked up at me. "Go on outside. This might take me a while."

I wrote down the passwords he needed and said, "We'll just be across the street in the playground if you need anything."

"Thanks."

I gave his shoulder a squeeze of gratitude as I turned to take Wendy outside.

We played for about a half hour, then David walked out the front door of our apartment and strode across the street.

I felt a rush of anxiety, because I had no idea what he was about to tell me. As he drew closer, I saw that he was frowning.

"**D**id you find something?" I asked as he reached me. Wendy was amusing herself on top of the play structure. There were no other children around.

"Maybe," he said, "but I'm not sure. What I found wasn't actually hidden anywhere. It was in Alex's regular email account, but in the deleted items. I just stumbled across it."

"What was it?"

He glanced uneasily up at Wendy. "Maybe it's nothing, but did Alex ever mention 'Vintage Car Chick' to you? Do you know who that might be?"

I slowly shook my head. "No."

His eyes met mine and he hesitated. "Then I don't know if I should show you this right now."

My stomach turned over. "Why not now? Please, David. I can take it."

Reluctantly he reached into his shirt pocket, pulled out a folded piece of paper and handed it to me. "I printed it for you."

I unfolded it and noted that it was dated only a few days before Alex died. The sender's email address was listed as vintagecarchick@—.

I quickly began to read.

Hi Alex. I feel unbelievably happy today and can't tell you how much it meant to me that you drove so far to see me last night. I wasn't sure what to expect when I told you about the baby, but you were amazing. It means so much to me to know that I can count on you. I was scared last night and I know I said some crazy things, but now I have no doubt that this child is going to be the luckiest girl in the world to have you in her life.

I know you want to keep our relationship secret for now, and I understand why. You want to protect your family and I admire you for that. I promised last night that I would respect that wish. I'm just glad I found you.

Love Carla

My breath caught in my throat and I couldn't speak or move. I feared I might pass out.

"Are you okay?" David asked with concern.

My chest heaved. "I'm not sure. I'd like to hit something right now."

He waited patiently for me to process what I'd read.

"Did Alex reply to this?" I asked, lifting my watery gaze. "And were there any other emails from her?"

"That was the only one I found," David replied. "And I searched through all the laptop files. I also searched Twitter and Facebook, but I didn't find anyone to match up with the 'Vintage Car Chick' handle." He paused and raked a hand through his hair. "God, Audrey, this is hard. Part of me wasn't even sure if I should tell you about this. And I'm just as shocked as you are."

"Did he reply?" I asked again.

At last, David nodded. "Do you want to see that email, too?"

My stomach muscles clenched. "Yes."

This time he reached into the back pocket of his jeans and pulled out another folded piece of paper from my home printer.

Clearly, David had given a great deal of thought to how he was going to present these emails to me.

I unfolded the second email and read that one as well.

Hi Carla. I was happy to see you last night, too. Everything makes sense to me now. But it's really important that you don't email me at this address. Please use my work email, at least for the time being. I promise I'll figure everything out soon. Just give me some time. It's not going to be easy to hurt people I care about. I'm glad you understand. I'll call you tonight.
Alex
xoxo

Lowering the page to my side, I tipped my head back and looked up at the sky.

Everything I believed in, everything I cared about, seemed to be crashing down on top of me.

"This can't be happening." I watched a fluffy white cloud move in front of the sun. "For two years I've been grieving the loss of my beloved husband—a man I wanted to believe was faithful and honorable. Now it all seems like a lie."

I met David's sympathetic gaze and was glad he was here, because I desperately needed to vent my emotions.

"I feel like he just died all over again," I continued. "This is exactly like the moment Dr. O'Brien walked into the supply room and told me that Alex's brain was pulverized and there was no hope. It was so hard to accept that—but here I am again, two years later, hearing horrible news about the man I married, and there's nothing I can do about it. I'm completely powerless." I waved an arm through the air. "I can't even march down to the station right now and slap him across the face or yell at him. He's gone, and I won't be able to deal with this. I'll never get an explanation from him. How am I going to cope?"

The next thing I knew, David was holding me in his arms and I was bawling like a baby, sobbing uncontrollably into his chest.

Then I felt a tug on the bottom of my shirt. I stepped back and looked down at my daughter. Her tiny brow was furrowed with concern. "What's the matter, Mommy?"

Quickly, I wiped the tears from my eyes and squatted down to answer her question. "I'm just sad about your daddy," I told her.

Pulling her close, I picked her up and rose to my feet. What a comfort it was, to feel her legs wrap around my hips and her arms clutch my neck.

David laid a hand on my shoulder. "I'm sorry, Audrey," he softly said. "And I want to help you."

All I could do was nod my head.

Together we walked back to the house.

Thank God for David. When we returned to the apartment, he played with Wendy in the living room, which gave me a chance to collect myself. While they sat on the floor and built a house out of LEGO blocks, I withdrew to my bedroom to lie down and stare at the ceiling for a while.

I must have laid there for an hour, replaying dozens of memories in my mind...the day Alex proposed on the bridge in the park...all the times he took me driving in the Buick, and how we had worked so passionately on my Mustang in those early days of our relationship.

Then there was Melanie...the psycho girlfriend who tried to burn me alive.

During that hour, alone in my bedroom, I relived many moments, good and bad, and secretly wished I'd never found that picture in the glove box of Alex's father's old car. If I'd had a choice, I would have preferred to live the rest of my days in total ignorance.

But as the time slowly passed, I began to think again.

It was the picture that stuck with me.

The ultrasound of that unborn baby.

When I finally emerged from my bedroom, the sun had set and David was in the kitchen with Wendy. He was at the stove cooking macaroni and cheese while she sat at the table, counting out baby carrots to arrange on a platter.

"Hey there," I said, moving to kiss her on the forehead. "Are you putting out enough for me, too?"

"Yes," she replied. "David said we needed twenty."

"And you can count to twenty, can't you?" he said.

"I learned how at Judy's," she told him.

David turned to me with his eyebrows raised. "Who's Judy?"

"Judy's Pre-school," I explained. "They're wonderful there. Best pre-school a working mother could ask for."

I joined him at the stove where he was holding a wooden spoon, stirring the pasta in a pot of steaming water.

"Sorry," he quietly said, "I didn't know what else to cook. She said she liked macaroni."

"It's perfect," I replied. "I really appreciate you staying. I hope I'm not ruining your plans for tonight."

"What plans?" There was a hint of humor in his tone that was obviously intended to make me feel better about keeping him here.

It wasn't easy to return his smile, however, because my eyes were puffy and hideous, but I gave it my best shot as I went in search of the colander.

I told David he didn't have to, but he insisted on staying while I put Wendy to bed. He said he wanted to do some more work on my laptop, which of course meant that he was going to continue searching for information about Carla, the Vintage Car Chick.

After I flicked the switch on Wendy's bedside lamp, I returned to the kitchen where David was seated at the table with the laptop open.

"Is she asleep?" he asked.

"Not yet, but it won't take long. We just read a story and she always drifts off pretty fast."

I stood up on my tiptoes to open the cupboard over the stove and found a bottle of whiskey that was stashed up there. "Tonight, I could use a drink," I said. "Want one?"

"Sounds good," he replied.

I set the bottle on the counter and opened the freezer. "Do you want ice with it? Or I could mix it with some ginger ale."

"Straight up," he replied. "But go easy on me. I'm driving."

"Don't worry, I'm an ER nurse," I reminded him. "I won't even let you touch your keys if there are refills."

I poured an ounce of whisky in each of two heavy crystal glasses Alex and I had received as a wedding gift. It was a rather poignant moment, considering I'd never used them before. Not once. I'd been keeping them for a special occasion because they were so gorgeous.

Who had given them to us? I had to think for a moment. *Was it David?* I believed it was.

I turned and carried the drinks to the table. "Do these look familiar to you?"

He inspected his glass, then held it high to clink against mine. "Yes, they do. Here's to Alex."

His unexpected toast to honor my cheating husband caught me off guard, and I froze. After a few heart-wrenching seconds, I raised my glass, clinked it against his—because I couldn't leave him hanging—but then I set my drink down on the table without sipping any.

"Were you able to find anything else?" I asked.

David shook his head. "Nothing. And you already checked his phone?"

"Yes."

David stared at the screen for a few more seconds, then closed the laptop. "While you were putting Wendy to bed, I tried emailing the 'Vintage Car Chick' email address, but my message bounced back. The account must have been closed, and there's nothing else here. I can check at the station computer tomorrow if you like, and I'll see if I can find out if Alex was taking a course to upgrade his certification."

"I already know that's not true." I took the first sip of my whiskey and winced at the scalding sensation that seared my throat. "Maybe you shouldn't even bother."

"It's worth checking out," David replied. "If he really was taking a course, it'll help you to know that."

I sighed and leaned back in my chair. "In the playground, you said you were shocked by this. I hate to admit it, but I'm *not*, and that just makes me feel like a fool."

"Why?"

"Because I made the decision to marry Alex when I had doubts from the beginning."

"What kind of doubts?"

I gave him a look. "Don't you remember that first day he showed up in the ER? You were there. He flirted with me like there was no tomorrow and took off his shirt when I asked him to take off his shoe. Right away, I sensed he was a skirt-chaser. Then he asked me out and I said no because alarm bells were going off in my head. But he was persistent and charming, and eventually I simply gave in."

David raised his drink to his lips. "I won't lie. Alex did enjoy the single life before he met you. He had a knack for attracting pretty women, but it was different with you. He was totally smitten because you weren't like the others. You actually had a brain."

I scoffed. "Obviously not much of one, because I fell backwards, head over heels, because of that relentless charm."

"He was more than just a charmer and you know it," David said. "He was my best friend, and I trusted him with my life. And despite what you think, I know he loved you."

I frowned and shook my head as if to clear it. "Why are you defending him? You saw the email and the picture of the baby. You saw me cry my eyes out a few hours ago. At the moment, I hope he's burning in hell."

David stared at me for a long moment. "You don't mean that, Audrey."

"He was *cheating* on me," I reminded him.

David leaned back in his chair. "I have one word to say to you, and it's the only thing that will get you through this."

"What's that?"

"Forgiveness," he replied.

I was tempted to roll my eyes but I resisted.

"You can't live the rest of your days feeling bitter and spiteful," David continued. "It'll eat you up inside and keep you from enjoying the good things that will come your way later on. And there *will* be good things, I promise you that."

"That's easy for you to say," I replied, raising my glass to my lips. "You weren't the one who was cheated on."

He breathed deeply. "Maybe so. But I do know that Alex was a good father, a good friend and a damn good firefighter. He saved a lot of lives in his career, so I think he earned a ticket to heaven, even if he made some mistakes. We all make them, and you still don't know the whole story here. Maybe he had a relationship with this woman before he met you. Maybe the ultrasound picture was taken five years ago and she only wrote the date on the back when she met with him. We haven't connected all the dots yet."

A lump the size of a boiled egg formed in my throat as another wave of guilt washed over me. But I didn't want to feel guilt. I wasn't the one who'd cheated. All these unmanageable, colliding feelings made me want to throw my glass against the wall, but I didn't want to destroy David's extravagant gift and wake Wendy up in the process.

"Why do I feel so guilty when *he* was the one who was cheating?"

David reached across the table and laid his hand on my wrist. "Let's give him the benefit of the doubt, at least until we find out more."

I shook my head in defeat. "Clearly you're an optimist, but I just can't see it that way. You read the emails. I think I'd be deluding myself if I let myself believe there was some other explanation. And here's the thing: I always had a feeling there would be unexpected surprises down the road. I knew it wasn't going to be easy to be Alex's wife because he was so attractive. Sure...everything was great in the beginning when we were newlyweds, but when I had that miscarriage, life wasn't as sunny as it was when we first got together. Maybe it was partly my fault. I was depressed for a while."

I tipped my glass up and emptied it.

"All couples go through rough times," David said.

Rising to my feet, I fetched the whisky bottle off the counter and carried it back to the table where I refilled my glass.

"I'm not driving anywhere," I assured him with a small grin as I settled back into my chair. For a while, we sat in silence.

"So what about *you?*" I asked. "Have you gone through any rough times with your lady friend? I apologize, I can't remember her name."

"Cheryl?" he asked. He shook his head. "We're not together anymore, so I guess you could say yes, we went through some rough times."

"I'm sorry to hear that," I said. "Guess it's my day to put my foot in it."

"Don't worry about it," David replied. "She had a job prospect in Texas, wanted to take it, and I didn't want to leave Manchester. It all worked out for the best. She said it was the wake-up call she needed, because neither of us was willing to budge for the other person. I'm just glad we found out sooner rather than later."

I took another sip of whisky. "Why didn't you want to leave Manchester? Was it your job here? Or the Texas heat that held you back?"

He thought about it for a moment. "It was more than that. For the right person, I'd move anywhere. She just wasn't the right one, I guess, and I wasn't the right one for her either, or she would have stayed."

I ran the palm of my hand over the smooth table top to whisk away a few crumbs from dinner. "Funny how you just know," I said. "And it might surprise you to hear this, but despite everything, if I could go back, I don't think I would do anything differently with Alex, because then I wouldn't have Wendy. The past two years were definitely rough, but we're doing better now. I wouldn't want to change a thing."

"Well, there you go," David gently said. "I've always believed that when things seem about as bad as they can get, there's usually *something* good that comes out of it. You just have to wait to understand what it is."

"You're right," I replied. "But I can't imagine how finding out that my husband was cheating on me could ever be a good thing. It's just going to destroy my memory of him, and I don't want that to happen."

"Wisdom comes with time," David said.

I tapped my fingernail on the shiny crystal glass. "Would you like some chips?"

He laughed at the abrupt change in subject. "Sure."

I got up and rifled through the bottom cupboard for a bag and poured it into a big plastic bowl. Returning to the table, I set it down between us.

"I'd really appreciate it if you could search the station computer for Miss Vintage Car Chick tomorrow, because wisdom is eluding me at the moment. All I feel is pain, and anger."

"We'll work on that," David replied as he reached into the chip bowl.

I wasn't scheduled to work the following day which turned out to be a blessing, because when it came to cheap whisky, I was obviously a lightweight. Morning brought with it a punishing headache that made me promise never to drink hard liquor again.

On top of that, I could barely remember what happened when David left. I knew we'd moved into the living room, turned on the TV and talked until midnight. Most of it was a blur, but I could at least recall that we spent a great deal of time reminiscing about Alex. David had known him far longer than I, and he shared many fond memories from their youth. All the things he admired about Alex were the same things I'd always admired.

One thing I *did* remember. When it was time for David to go, I hugged him at the door and thanked him profusely for being such a good friend.

"You're drunk," he'd said with a laugh.

I have a vague recollection of stumbling backward into the wall and knocking a framed picture off kilter. David straightened it for me before he left and told me to get some sleep. He promised to call me in the morning.

So here I sat on the sofa, sipping an extra-large cup of coffee while Wendy bounced and danced on the carpet to The Wiggles.

"Hot potato, hot potato…"

Oh, to have that much energy again.

The phone rang and I realized I had more energy than I thought. I practically dove across the sofa to answer it.

"Hello?"

"Hi Audrey. It's David."

My heart came alive, because there were still so many unanswered questions in my mind, and David was my best hope to resolve them. "Hey," I said.

"How are you feeling this morning?" he asked. "Is the room spinning?"

I laughed. "A little bit, yeah. Though I'm not sure if it's the hangover or the fact that Wendy is watching *The Wiggles* right now. Boy, that's one colorful TV show."

"The music's kind of addictive, isn't it?" he replied. "I watched it once with my nephew and I couldn't get that "Rock-A-Bye Your Bear" song out of my head for days. Seriously, I lost sleep, and I still know every word."

"They're musical geniuses." Raising my coffee to my lips, I took another sip.

"Have you ever taken Wendy to see them perform live?" David asked. "You should, next time they're in New York."

"She'd love that," I replied.

He was quiet for a moment, and I sipped my coffee while The Wiggles continued to sing.

"I can't help wondering why you're calling," I finally said, wanting to give David a nudge—though I wasn't sure I wanted to hear what he might say. Not if it concerned Alex and his personal emails on the station computer. But I knew I had to face it.

"I came in early," he told me, "to check through some old files."

"Thanks for doing that," I replied. "Did you find anything?"

He let out a sigh. "Sorry. Everything was purged awhile back so I couldn't get at Alex's emails, but I did ask the chief whether or not he'd been taking a course to upgrade his certification. The chief had no record of it."

Though I wasn't surprised to hear that, it still felt like a punch in the stomach. I tipped my head back onto the sofa cushion. "I appreciate you telling me." I couldn't seem to form any other words.

"Are you okay?" he asked.

I swallowed hard over a lump in my throat. "I'm not sure. I just wish he'd told me the truth or I had probed a little harder when he started acting differently. I suggested he go see a doctor, but that was it. I just let it go. Now I'll never get the chance to talk to him about it."

"I'm sorry, Audrey," David said. "I wish there was something I could do."

"Don't apologize. You've been wonderful. I just have to figure out where to go from here. Do I just let it lie and try to forget about it, focus on the good stuff? Or do I keep digging?"

I could hear the familiar sounds of the fire station in the background—voices of the other men laughing about something.

"Do you want my opinion?" David asked.

"Of course."

"I don't think you'll be able to live without knowing the truth. You'll go mad."

I nodded. "You're probably right. But the only person who would have the answers I need is Carla, and how in the world am I supposed to find her? All we had to go on was her email address but that no longer exists. I'd love to hire a private investigator but I can't afford it."

"I'll help you," David said. "There's got to be a way. First off, didn't you and Alex get into the vintage car scene when you were working on your Mustang? I remember him mentioning going to a car rally once."

I sat up. "Yes, and we went into a few chat rooms looking for answers to some questions."

"Do you remember the sites?" David asked. "Maybe Vintage Car Chick is still around, chatting up other women's husbands."

I couldn't help but smile. "You're bad." But then my smile faded as I thought about that. "When do you think they got together? I mean…if she told him she was pregnant the week before he died, obviously they must have been together months before that. I can't bear to think about it."

"Then, don't," David said. "You'll drive yourself crazy."

"And how do we know it's even Alex's kid?" I asked. "What if she was sleeping around?"

"That's a good point, and you can prove anything these days through a simple DNA test," David replied, "if it comes to that."

"That's good to know. But if Alex really was the father of her child, why didn't she come forward and try to contact us after he died? She might have been able to sue for a portion of his estate and get child support. He didn't have a lot of insurance, but he did have some."

David considered that. "These are all valid questions you need answered. We have to keep digging."

I liked how he said "we." It made me feel less alone. Less crazy.

"I need to get back to work now," he said, "but I'll come by later if you want. I have some ideas about where we can start looking."

"I'd love that, thank you, and will you stay for supper? I promise it won't be mac 'n' cheese."

"A home cooked meal?" he replied. "I can't say no to that."

We hung up, and by some coincidence, the "Rock-a-bye Your Bear" song came on *The Wiggles Show*. I sang along with Wendy and realized I knew every word, too.

After taking care of all the prep work for dinner, I took Wendy outside to play until David arrived. On that particular afternoon, there were some other children on the structure and she was quick, as always, to make friends. Two mothers stood on the far side of the park, deeply engaged in conversation.

I sat alone on the bench, keeping an eye out for David on the street. Before long he pulled up in a shiny new silver Hyundai Tucson and got out.

"David!" I called. "We're over here!"

He spotted me, waited for a car to pass, then jogged across the street. Dressed in faded blue jeans and a gray cotton button-down shirt, he sat down on the bench beside me.

"How are you doing?" he asked.

"I'm all right. You?"

"I'm good. It was a quiet day at work, and that's always a good thing." I felt his gaze on me as I smiled and clapped for Wendy, who came squealing down the big swirly slide.

"You look better today," he mentioned.

I slid a playful glance his way. "Compared to last night? That's probably not saying much. I apologize if I was a drunken slob."

He chuckled. "Hey, don't apologize. You were funny."

"Well, I guess that's better than pathetic," I cheerfully replied.

He patted my knee, then shouted a cheer for Wendy when she coasted down the slide again. We watched her for a few minutes, then I crossed my legs and rested my arm along the back of the bench.

"You know…" I said, feeling as if there was so much to say, "I've been thinking about everything since yesterday, and I'm at least glad this is happening now, two years after losing Alex. Wendy and I have managed to get used to living without him—practically anyway—and the wounds aren't quite so raw. If I'd found out about this a year ago, it would have been a lot tougher."

He watched Wendy with a wistful expression. "It's never easy to lose someone you love," he said, "but time is the best healer."

I regarded him curiously. "Have you ever lost someone? Besides Alex, I mean?"

"Yeah," he said. "My mom died five years ago. She got sick, and it happened pretty quickly."

"What was wrong with her, if you don't mind my asking?"

David kept his eyes fixed on Wendy who was now scrambling up the ladder while the other children followed. "It was a brain tumor," he explained. "By the time they found it, she only had a month to live."

"Oh, God, I'm so sorry."

"She was a good mom," he said. "I miss her a lot, but in some ways, I feel like she's still around, looking out for me." He touched his fist to his chest and turned his eyes to meet mine. "She's in here."

Like a flash flood of emotion, my eyes grew wet and my throat ached. The pain spread all the way to my ears, but I took a breath and maintained my composure. "I wish I could have met her."

He nodded. "Yeah, you would have liked her."

We sat together in silence, watching Wendy play. David leaned forward with his elbows on his knees while I glanced over at the other mothers who were spreading a blanket out on the grass.

I blinked a few times as I watched them—remembering another time—then let out a puff of air. *"Huh."*

David leaned back to look at me. "What is it?"

I touched a finger to my lips. "I'm just remembering a day about a year ago when Wendy and I came out here to play. There was another little girl here and I spoke to her mother for quite a while. It felt odd at the time, because after I told her I was a widow, she asked a lot of questions about Alex. She seemed really curious." I tried to recall more of our conversation.

"How old was her daughter?" David asked.

My heart began to beat faster. "Just over a year old, toddling around the park, which means she would have been born not long before Alex died."

David leaned into me. "Did the woman tell you her name?"

I shook my head. "No, and I didn't tell her mine. She wasn't from around here, though. I remember that much. She said she was just passing through. I can't recall where she said she was from…" I wracked my brain to summon that detail, but it was lost to me.

I turned my gaze to David's. "Do you think it was her? Do you think she might have come to get a look at Wendy and me?"

I couldn't help myself. Having been the object of a female stalker in the past, I looked around the neighborhood, feeling as if I were being watched.

With a genuine expression of sympathy, David massaged my shoulder. "I don't know."

"There was definitely something weird about her," I said. "The way she looked at me…"

"I don't suppose you got her license plate number," he asked.

"No, but I do remember that she was driving something new. It wasn't anything vintage. I would have noticed that."

Wendy came running over to us. "I'm hungry," she said.

"Me, too," I replied. "Let's go make supper."

David and I stood up, and Wendy took hold of both our hands. She walked between us as we crossed the street and climbed the stairs to the apartment.

The phone was ringing as I unlocked the door. I had to hurry inside to answer it. "Hello?"

"Hi Audrey. It's Jean."

"Oh hi, Jean," I replied in a friendly tone as I sat down on the sofa. Covering the mouthpiece with my hand, I whispered to Wendy, "It's Grandma Jean."

"Can I say hi?" Wendy asked.

"Sure." I removed my hand to speak to Jean. "Wendy's right here and she'd like to say hello." I handed the phone over and watched her speak to her grandmother for a few minutes. Occasionally I glanced at David who was waiting patiently in the kitchen.

Wendy handed the phone back to me.

"Why don't you go ask David to get you some juice?" I whispered to her.

"Okay."

She ran to the kitchen and I put the phone back to my ear.

"Hi again," I said to Jean. "How have you been?"

"I'm fine," she replied, "but mostly I'm calling to see how *you're* doing. You left in such a hurry the other day. I was worried about you."

Nervous butterflies swarmed into my belly because I didn't feel ready to have this conversation with my mother-in-law. How could I tell her that her son might have been carrying on an affair with another woman before he died, and gotten the other woman pregnant?

I still didn't even know if what I suspected was true, so I couldn't possibly bring it up.

"I'm sorry about that," I said. "It was a rough day. There were a lot of memories welling up."

"I understand," she said. "We all felt the same way, and that's another reason why I'm calling."

I shifted uneasily on the sofa. "Really? What's going on?"

After a brief pause, Jean began to explain. "I didn't tell you this before, but I recently went through the Organ Donor Network to send a note to the person who received Alex's heart two years ago."

This piece of news hit me like a plank across the chest. I felt the vibration inside myself, and my eyebrows lifted. "What did you say in the note?"

"I wrote that I'd like to get together so we could meet in person," she replied.

I wasn't sure how I might have felt about this a week ago— before I found the ultrasound in the glove box of Alex's Buick— but today I felt an inexplicable bitterness toward the stranger who was walking around with my husband's cheating heart. It wasn't rational, I knew that. It wasn't the recipient's fault that Alex had acted like a jerk and betrayed his wife and child.

I wondered suddenly if I was going to require therapy after all this. It was just so complicated, from an emotional point of view.

"I didn't think you wanted that," I reminded Jean. "When you received that letter of thanks from her not long after Alex died, you said it was too painful. You didn't want to have any contact."

"It was painful back then," she explained, "but I think enough time has passed. I feel differently now. I'd like to meet all the people who received something from Alex. I want to see how he helped them. As a mother, it would make me very proud."

I closed my eyes and pinched the bridge of my nose. If Alex was having an affair, I wasn't certain I'd *ever* want to tell Jean. She idolized her son. She thought he was a hero in every sense of the word. It would break her heart to know the truth.

Then again, the child in that ultrasound photo could possibly be Jean's granddaughter. *Wouldn't it be wrong to deny her that knowledge?*

"I've invited the donor recipient to come for lunch next weekend," Jean told me. "Would you like to come, too?"

Again, butterflies invaded my belly and they seemed in an angry tizzy today. I felt shaken. Confused.

Realizing I had to choose my words carefully, I took a few seconds to clear my throat. "I don't think so, Jean. It's not something I want to do. At least not right now."

The long silence on the other end of the line made my heart feel heavy.

"Life does go on, Audrey," Jean finally said. "We have to keep going, and I'm sure Alex wouldn't have wanted you to pine away forever. He'd want you to move on and find happiness."

Believe me, I have every intention of moving on—just as soon as I dig up the past and take a good hard look at it with a magnifying glass.

That's right. I had no intention of letting my husband's infidelity break me or ruin the rest of my life. I had a beautiful daughter to raise and a job I loved. I deserved happiness like anyone else.

I just needed to know the truth first.

"Let me know how it goes," I said to Jean. "I hope it's a good experience for you, but I don't think I can be there." Then suddenly I felt a need to soften my rejection. Quickly I added, "And I think I'm working that day anyway."

I could hear the disappointment in her voice. "Okay. I understand. But bring Wendy over soon, all right? We miss her."

"Of course."

With that, I hung up and pushed myself off the sofa to go cook dinner for my guest.

That night, after I put Wendy to bed, David and I sat at the computer in the living room, searching through old car restoration websites and community forums for Vintage Car Chick. We didn't find a single thing, but we did venture into our individual Facebook pages. He showed me old videos and pictures he'd posted years ago when he first started his page.

I played some obscure music for him—indie artists I loved that were off the beaten track—and he played me a number of contemporary bluesy tunes I'd never heard before.

It was nearly eleven when we said good night. This time I was sober because I had to work in the morning. I didn't throw my arms around him as I did the night before, but he surprised me by leaning forward and giving me a friendly kiss on the cheek. "I'll call you tomorrow night," he said.

As I locked the door behind him, I stood for a moment in the hall, unable to wipe the smile off my face.

It had been a fun evening—which was definitely something I'd needed.

At four o'clock in the morning, I woke from a terrible nightmare.

In the dream, I was sitting in the back seat of the Buick and Alex was driving. In the front seat, beside him, was the woman from the park—the one who had asked me all the personal questions about him.

They laughed and joked about things I didn't understand. Everything they said sounded garbled—like the teacher's voice in the Charlie Brown cartoons—but I knew they were having a good time. They didn't seem the slightest bit conscious of the fact that I was present in the car.

I felt invisible and jealous of their connection, and soon my rage escalated to such a state, I began to shout and pound on the glass between the back seat and the front—which was odd because there was no interior window inside the Buick.

Alex and the woman—I'll just call her Carla—turned around to stare at me in horror, as if I were a crazed chainsaw murderer. Then Alex slammed on the brakes and they both flew forward through the front windshield, passing through it as if it weren't even there. They disappeared into the sky, like Keanu Reeves at the end of *The Matrix* and I was left in the back seat all alone.

I was wearing my seatbelt. Obviously they hadn't been.

I woke in a cold sweat, filled with raging emotions. I couldn't shake the frustration that lingered from pounding my fists on the glass while I was powerless to break through and tell Alex how I felt. He couldn't hear me.

I wanted to scream, but I kept my mouth shut because Wendy was asleep in the next room.

Never once during my marriage had I ever felt such anger toward my husband.

I wanted him back, alive again, standing in front of me, so that I could shake him, yell at him and tear a good long strip off of him. Because he deserved it. Oh, how he deserved it.

Perhaps you'll think I'm stupid when you hear the next part of this story. I certainly felt like an idiot when things transpired as they did. Not long afterward, I wondered if I should get my brain checked.

I'm not sure what made me forget that my mother-in-law had invited the recipient of Alex's heart for lunch the following Saturday. She'd also invited me to attend, but I had declined because I was too angry with Alex and didn't have the heart to explain why—pardon the pun. Over the next few days I was so absorbed in my own problems and unlocking the mystery of "Carla, Vintage Car Chick," that I didn't give much thought to my mother-in-law's important luncheon.

David and I both worked heavy shifts that week, so we only spoke a few times on the phone. I also spoke to Cathy, and like the good friend she was, she listened to me rail on and on about what had occurred since I found the ultrasound photo in the Buick.

I should have known better than to wallow in my anger—I was usually more in control of my emotions—but I needed to blow off some steam, so that's what I did.

By Saturday, there was nothing left to say about it and I hadn't uncovered any additional information, so when Wendy asked if we could visit Grandma, I suggested we pop by after we finished grocery shopping.

Maybe there was some intuition involved—either on Wendy's part or mine. I'll never know, but it was interesting how so many of the puzzle pieces came together on that day. It makes me wonder about the possibility of fate.

When I pulled over at the curb near Jean's driveway, I couldn't believe what I was seeing. Frowning, I gripped the steering wheel with both hands and squinted through the hazy, late afternoon sunshine.

Yes, it was real. It wasn't a dream.

"Stay here, sweetie," I said to Wendy, who was buckled into the booster seat in the back.

Flicking the door handle, I stepped out of my vehicle and approached the car that was parked in front of mine.

A woman was bent over, buckling her own child into the back. I had to wait a moment on the sidewalk until she finished. When at last she straightened and turned to face me, my stomach pitched and rolled like a small boat on a large wave.

"*You...*" I said to her—to the very same woman who had found me in the playground across the street from my home a year ago. The woman who had asked far too many personal questions about my relationship with my dead husband.

As I stood in front of Jean's home, I felt violated, not unlike the night I stood on the road watching my house burn to the ground because a female stalker, obsessed with my husband, had wanted me out of the way.

A look of recognition flickered in the woman's eyes and she took a breath. "I'm sorry," she said. "This is awkward."

"I'll say."

What was she doing here? Had she come to present herself to Jean as Alex's one *true* love?

"What are you doing here?" I asked, my tone dripping with accusation.

"I came to meet Jean and Garry," she replied. "They invited me."

"They *did*? My God." I wished suddenly that I had confided in Jean on the phone and told her the truth about Alex and the picture I'd found in the car.

Who knows what this woman might have said to them. I didn't trust her one iota because she'd already proven she lacked integrity. That had become obvious the moment she slept with another woman's husband and was eager to become a home wrecker.

I looked down at the little girl in the car and shivered at the possibility that she might belong to Alex. Did she have his eyes? His smile?

Then I noticed a man sitting in the driver's seat. He leaned across the passenger seat with his head tilted to look up at me.

He was curious. Probably because I was speaking in heated tones.

"Who's that?" I quietly asked, feeling daunted all of a sudden because I was standing on the street, on my own, boldly confronting the woman who may have slept with my husband.

I wished David was there so I had some support. I also wished I didn't feel like one of those jealous wives who scream and point fingers on the *Maury Povich Show*. *Please, don't let me be that.*

"He's my husband," the woman replied. "His name is Jesse. And you're Audrey...right?"

The woman's eyes were warm and friendly, surprisingly sympathetic.

"Yes," I said, feeling confused and unsettled by her knowledge of me. "And you're Carla?"

She pursed her lips questioningly and grinned at me. "No, I'm Nadia. We met a year ago in the playground across the street from your house." She held out her hand to shake mine. "I'm sorry I didn't tell you who I was back then. I probably should have, but I was embarrassed that I'd violated the confidentiality agreement. I kind of felt like a stalker."

I was in a daze as I looked down at her outstretched hand… realizing slowly that this was not the woman who had borne a child with my husband. This was the person who had received his heart on the day he died.

Good God. What was wrong with me?

My gaze lifted to her chest where I saw the top of a scar. "You're the heart recipient," I said, slipping my hand into hers.

It was mind-boggling to me, that Alex's heart was actually beating inside this woman who stood before me. An organ from his living form was pumping blood through her body, keeping her alive—yet he was gone. As a physical being, he no longer existed in this world.

"Yes, that's me," she replied as we shook hands.

"I'm an idiot," I said. "I'm so sorry."

"Sorry for what?" she asked. "I can understand why you'd be reluctant to meet me, and I was worried about meeting you today. I didn't know how to explain myself. I shouldn't have pried into your life the way I did last year, without telling you who I was."

"I thought you were someone else," I blurted out.

She shook her head with confusion.

"Never mind," I said. "It was a stupid mistake." I wanted to sink through the concrete.

"Are you leaving now?" I asked, glancing down at her daughter in the back seat and suddenly wishing I had accepted Jean's invitation, because I didn't want this woman to go yet.

"Yes," she replied. "We were here all afternoon and Ellen is pretty tuckered out, but I'm sorry I didn't get a chance to spend more time with you."

Her husband got out of the car. "Hi," he said, circling around the back. "You must be Audrey."

He was young and handsome and was dressed casually in jeans and a long sleeved gray T-shirt.

Nadia gestured toward him. "This is my husband, Jesse."

Holding out a hand to shake his, I said, "It's nice to meet you. And is this your daughter? She's gotten bigger since the last time I saw her."

"They grow so fast," Nadia said. She bent forward to speak to the little girl. "Ellen, say hi to Audrey. We met her last year in the playground in Manchester. Do you remember?"

Ellen nodded, but she looked as if she was about to nod off, and I suspected she didn't remember me at all. She was just being polite, which displayed incredibly good social skills for a two-year-old.

Jesse and Nadia stood on the sidewalk for a few seconds, their smiles full of warmth and curiosity. I was, after all, the wife of the man who saved Nadia's life.

Strangely, much of my anger toward Alex slipped away in that moment, and I felt as if he was actually here, standing on the sidewalk, showering me with love—not knowing, of course, that I'd wanted to tear a strip off him all week. Or maybe he did know and wasn't fazed by it.

But that was silly. He wasn't here.

Nadia reached over to lay a hand on my arm. "Are you okay? You look a little pale."

Her touch was comforting. I struggled to breathe evenly. "It's been a strange week," I replied. "And I wish I had come to lunch today. I didn't want to meet you before, but I think I was in some kind of denial. Now that we're face to face, I don't want you to go."

Nadia looked up at her husband. Their gazes held for a moment, then he said, "Why don't you two hang out for a while? I can take Ellen for a drive around town until she falls asleep. Want me to drop you off at a bar or something?" he suggested with a smile.

I gestured toward my car where Wendy was waiting patiently. "I have my daughter. We were just going to visit Jean and Garry, but I could ask if they'd mind watching her for a bit. Then we could take my car," I said to Nadia.

"That sounds perfect," she replied. "I'll wait for you here."

Quickly I went to get Wendy out of her booster seat, and felt incredibly exhilarated. I wasn't sure what was causing such euphoria, though I did hope there would be some answers today.

Answers to what questions, I wasn't sure, because this woman had never actually met my husband. How could she know anything?

Since I was driving—and Nadia had already enjoyed a few glasses of wine that afternoon—we opted for a nearby coffee shop.

After we sat down with our coffees, I asked her all sorts of questions about how she ended up needing a heart transplant in the first place. She told me about her illness, which resulted in a very high-risk pregnancy and delivery, and for a few brief moments it helped me forget about my husband's infidelity—because he had not only saved this woman's life, he'd also saved a newborn baby from becoming motherless. For that, I was proud.

Nadia had questions for me as well. She wanted to know how Alex and I had met, and I told her about all the good times, willing myself not to bring up any of my doubts or suspicions about his affair. *Just keep smiling. She doesn't need to know.*

Then I don't know what came over me. My voice broke and I had to stop. I couldn't speak and I was afraid I might break down.

Dropping my gaze to my lap, I fought to regain control.

"I'm so sorry," she said. "I know this must be difficult."

I nodded, then found myself unable to put on a brave face and lie to this woman. I'd felt a strong connection to her from the beginning—since the first time I met her in the playground, though I didn't understand why at the time. I still wasn't quite sure why I felt so at ease with her now, other than the fact that I knew she had my husband's heart.

Was that the reason? Was there something profound going on here? Or was she simply a person I would have been friends with, regardless?

Either way, I wanted her to know the truth today. I didn't want to be false.

Then she surprised me by asking...very gently, "Who did you think I was when you first approached me today? You called me Carla and you seemed upset."

My eyes lifted. Either Nadia was naturally intuitive or somehow Alex's heart was giving her extraordinary insight into my soul.

"I was," I replied. "I've been upset all week because something happened. It's why I didn't want to meet the recipient of my husband's heart."

She leaned forward over the table, her expression laced with sympathy.

"I found something in Alex's car," I explained.

"The Buick in his parents' garage?" she asked.

I nodded. "It was a picture of a baby, taken during an ultrasound. There was a note on the back dated a week before he died and it said, 'For Alex, I hope she has your good looks. Love Carla.' There was a little heart drawn in the corner."

Nadia's eyebrows pulled together with dismay. "So you think he was having an affair?"

Again, I nodded my head. "Two weeks before he died, he started acting differently. He was distracted and didn't come home at the normal times." I paused and gazed toward the windows. "It's driving me crazy—not knowing—and I haven't been able to tell Jean. It would break her heart to know her son was cheating, but I also think that if she has a grandchild out there somewhere, she'd want to know."

Nadia sat back in her chair. "God, I'm so sorry."

I returned my gaze to meet hers. "I've been really angry with him this week—and that's the real reason I didn't want to meet you today. I was afraid I might be tempted to throw a vase at you or something, because you have his heart. It's stupid, I know."

Her eyebrows lifted. "It's not stupid. I'd probably feel the same way if I found out something like that about Jesse."

I sighed heavily, then an image popped into my mind. "Gosh, I just remembered the dream I had last night. I was riding in the back seat of the Buick, and you were sitting in the front with Alex. I thought you were Carla because I remembered having met you last year and you were so curious about him. The two of you were laughing and joking, but I couldn't make out anything you were saying. I felt like I was intruding on your relationship, but now that I've met you, I can sort of understand why I had that dream—because the two of you do share something. The same heart."

"Wow," Nadia said, sitting back. "I've had a lot of strange dreams myself since the surgery. I was telling Jean about it today. That's how I figured out who Alex was, and how I found you in the playground last year. I knew his name even before the Donor Network connected me with Jean."

This fascinated me, and I leaned forward, resting my forearms on the table. "What kind of dreams have you had?" I asked.

She gave me a sheepish look. "I feel funny talking about it because it sounds so New Agey, but I've dreamed that I'm flying, sometimes over the transplant center, and once, a man flew beside me and he told me his name was Alex. I was really sick at the time, falling in and out of consciousness. I can't explain what it all means, but I like to think that he followed me in the ambulance to make sure I was okay." Nadia paused and chuckled softly. "Maybe somehow he felt his old heart racing out of control, because I was pretty scared."

I looked down at my coffee and confided, "I've had a lot of dreams of Alex, but he's always out of reach, sometimes with his back to me. I can never talk to him. Last night in the dream, there was a glass window between the front seat and the back. I've never had a sense that he was coming to check on me directly. It's the opposite— more that I'm trying to reach *him*, but I can't." I felt a little jealous that he might be checking on Nadia, but not Wendy and me.

Was he checking on Carla and her child?

Nadia waved a dismissive hand. "They're just dreams," she said as if she recognized my anguish. "And are you really sure he was having an affair? Do you know who this Carla person is, or *where* she is? If you could talk to her and find out the truth, it might help you deal with it."

I hooked my fingers through the handle of my coffee mug and raised it to my lips. "That's the problem. I don't know her last name and we have no contact information."

"Who's *we*?" Nadia asked.

"My friend David," I replied. "Actually, he was Alex's best friend. I'm sure he'd like to meet you sometime, if you'd be willing."

"Of course I would be," she said with enthusiasm. Then she stared at me for a long moment, as if thinking carefully about something. "And I might be able to help you with your other problem. Do you really want to find this woman?"

I felt a great rush of anticipation. "Yes, definitely."

Nadia reached for her giant purse on the floor at her feet, plopped it on her lap and dug into it. After retrieving a pen and a small notepad, she pushed her coffee mug aside.

"I have a twin sister and she's a lawyer in Boston. She specializes in family law and uses private investigators all the time to catch cheating spouses, locate deadbeat dads…you name it. She might be able to find this Carla person. Do you know if she lives in Connecticut?"

"I'm not sure," I replied, "but we found an email from her where she used the name 'Vintage Car Chick.' The email account is no longer active, but it might be a starting point."

"That's helpful," Nadia said, writing it down. "So tell me everything you know about her and I can pass it on to Diana. I'll give you my email address and can you forward me that email when you get home?"

"Of course," I replied with a swell of elation, feeling amazed and grateful that fate had intervened and caused my path to intersect with the recipient of my late husband's heart.

Maybe that's where Alex was hiding all his secrets.

W hen I arrived home that night, the first thing I did after putting Wendy to bed was call David. The instant he picked up the phone and said hello, I told him that I'd met the recipient of Alex's heart that day.

"Don't say anything more," he quickly replied. "I'm coming right over."

I felt slightly breathless as I hung up. Then I dashed around the apartment, picking up clutter and loading dirty dishes into the dishwasher. Next I brushed my teeth, combed my hair and put on a little makeup.

I couldn't wait to see him and tell him everything that happened that day.

After a week of insecurity and emotional torment, I felt positively euphoric when David walked through the door. I rose up on my tip toes, threw my arms around his neck and hugged him.

I couldn't see his face but I could hear the laughter in his voice as he squeezed me in return. His arms were snug around my waist. "What's this for?"

"It was a great day," I replied, taking a step back to meet his sparkling blue-eyed gaze.

Tonight he wore loose-fitting jeans and a white cotton T-shirt. His golden hair was wavy and tousled. After such a satisfying, body-hugging embrace, I couldn't help but take in the attractive spectacle of his broad shoulders and muscular arms.

What is happening here?

"I'm glad to hear it," he replied, then peered down the hall. "Is Wendy asleep?"

"Yeah, she's out like a light. Come on in and I'll tell you everything."

Sweeping aside my awareness of his attractive masculinity—because my emotions were far too complicated right now and I didn't want to spoil what we had—I led him into the living room where we plunked ourselves down on the sofa.

I began with how I drove over to Jean's, pulled up behind Nadia, recognized her from the playground a year ago and thought she was Carla, Vintage Car Chick.

"That's unbelievable," David said after I told him that she was, in fact, someone else entirely.

His eyes glimmered with fascination, and I knew he shared my excitement over learning that the woman from the park wasn't a home-wrecking stalker. She was the person who had received Alex's heart.

It had been a long time since I'd felt so inspired talking to someone—except of course for Nadia, earlier that day—and I knew part of it stemmed from the fact that David loved Alex, too, and the idea of meeting the person who'd received his heart was both astounding and thrilling for both of us. Alex was gone, yet a part of him still lived and thrived in the world. I knew this meant as much to David as it did to me.

"I *would* like to meet her," he said, his gaze direct and intense. "When will you see her again?"

"I'm not sure yet," I replied. Then I explained how she offered to try and help us locate Carla. "I have to send Nadia an email tonight and forward the message Carla sent to Alex. I can arrange a meeting with her, if you want. She has a daughter which would be fun for Wendy because they could play together."

David waved a hand through the air. "Wait a second. I'm confused. I don't know much about science, but when did Nadia give birth to her daughter? Is it possible the kids share some DNA?"

I shook my head. "No. Ellen was delivered by C-section before Nadia had the transplant, so there's no connection there. But they liked each other when they met in the playground last year, and as a parent of an only child, I always want to help her make friends. Nadia's daughter is an only child, too, so Nadia feels the same way."

He nodded. "I get that. If you want to invite them over here, I could help you cook."

My whole face lit up and I smiled. "Okay."

David was quick to ask more questions. "So tell me more about her sister, the lawyer. She's her twin? How is she going to help us?"

I explained that Diana specialized in family law and she knew several of the best private investigators.

"I hope she can help us find some answers," David said.

"Me, too," I replied, happily aware of the fact that he had used the word "us" twice.

Forty-five

Together, David and I found the email from Vintage Car Chick and forwarded it to Nadia, then we invited her, Jesse and Ellen to come for dinner the following weekend.

Nadia replied five minutes later to inform me that she had already spoken to her sister on the phone and Diana was eager to roll up her sleeves and get to work. Rather than accept our invitation to dinner, however, Nadia countered with the suggestion that we come to her home in Waltham for a barbeque to meet Diana and her husband Jacob—a cardiac surgeon who worked at Boston Mass, and incidentally had treated Nadia before her transplant. Nadia also mentioned that they had just installed a nifty play structure in the yard for Ellen, and they were keen to put it to good use.

David and I accepted her invitation and couldn't wait to see where she lived. She had described her "blue house on the water" with great passion and affection.

I wanted to see it, because it was the place where a part of Alex now lived.

I'm not sure if Nadia asked her sister to make our case a top priority, but three days later I received an email from Diana directly.

I read it as soon as I came home from work, then I called David right away.

"I can't believe it," I said, staring at the computer screen, tapping my foot under the table. "It looks like they found her."

"You mean Carla?" he replied.

"Yes."

Wendy was in the living room, bouncing around to The Wiggles again.

"My God," David said. "Were they able to tell you anything about her?"

I took a deep breath as I read over the email for what felt like the hundredth time. "Her full name is Carla Christine Matthews. She lives in Boston and she's a waitress, but does some acting on the side. Mostly theater, but she's done some local commercials. She's a single mom—no big surprise there—and takes her daughter to a neighbor's house when she goes to work. All the information is right here, including her address, new email and phone number. There's even a photograph. I'm forwarding it to you now."

"Holy crap," he said. "They sure work fast. What does she look like?"

I swallowed uneasily. "It's hard to make out her features very well because the picture was taken from across a busy street and it's just a profile shot. It looks like she's walking fast, but I can tell her hair is blonde. I'd say she's about my age."

"Is her daughter with her?" David asked.

"No," I replied. "She's carrying grocery bags."

David was quiet for a moment, and I moved to the kitchen doorway to check on Wendy, who was still dancing in the living room.

"What are you going to do?" he asked.

"I'm not sure. What do *you* think I should do?"

He considered it. "That depends. Is this enough to satisfy your curiosity? Or do you want to meet her and find out if her daughter really does belong to Alex? If she is his child, it could complicate your life, not to mention open up a whole new can of worms in terms of child support from his estate."

I sat down at the kitchen table. "I don't care about that. I mean, I do care, but if she's Alex's daughter, that makes her Wendy's half-sister. I just want to do the right thing."

I ran my finger along a groove in the oak tabletop, waiting for David to say something. Then at last he spoke. "I admire you," he said. "You're a good person."

A pleasant warmth moved through me. "Thank you."

"And I know it's going to be tough," he continued, "but I want to help. I can come over if you want me to be there when you call, or I'll go with you to meet her."

"I think I'll start by sending her an email," I said.

"What are you going to say?" he asked.

"I'm not sure yet. I'll have to figure that out when I start typing."

As soon as I sat down to send an email to my late husband's mistress, I found it surprisingly easier than I thought it would be. I suppose, by that point, I just wanted to know the truth, and I believed I was getting close.

Dear Carla,

We've never met, but I think we may have something in common. My name is Audrey Fitzgerald and I was married to Alex Fitzgerald, a firefighter in Manchester, Connecticut who died on the job two years ago.

Recently I found a photo from a pregnancy ultrasound, and I think it may have been yours. I found it in the glove box of my husband's car. Does the photo belong to you? Did you know my husband?

I know this is an awkward question to ask, and I only want to know the truth about your relationship with him. I mean you no harm. I would very much appreciate hearing from you. You can either reply to this email or call me at the number below. If you would like to meet in person, I would be happy to come to Boston.

Sincerely,

Audrey

I debated whether or not I should delete the word "happy" to describe my feelings about meeting her—which wasn't entirely accurate—but I didn't want to scare her off. I believed that a friendly, non-threatening approach would yield the best results.

As soon as I hit send, I rested my elbows on the table and steepled my fingers together in front of my lips while I stared intensely at the computer screen. I waited about thirty seconds, then reverted to the Inbox, but there were no new messages.

I puttered around on Facebook for a while and checked the weather, then returned to my email program and opened the Inbox again.

No new messages.

Letting out a deep breath, I reminded myself that a watched pot never boils, so I forced myself to get up and do something else.

―⸲

A full twenty-four hours passed, and Carla Matthews did not respond to my email.

"What will I do if she doesn't reply at all?" I asked David on the phone that night after I put Wendy to bed. "And how long should I wait?"

I dropped an herbal teabag into a mug and poured hot water over it.

"You could always try calling her," he said, "or you could go to her house and knock on her door."

I turned to stare at the pile of papers on top of the large manila envelope on the kitchen table. "According to the information from the PI, she lives in a high-rise apartment building with a security entrance. So that might be easier said than done. I could always go to the restaurant where she works, but I don't know how she'd react. I'd hate to cause a scene in front of her boss."

One thing was certain, however. I couldn't just let it go. Not after coming this far. I needed to know if Alex had cheated on me, and if he was the father of another child. *Did Wendy have a half-sister?*

"Can I ask you something?" David said. "Last night you mentioned you wanted to do the right thing and you said it was important for you to know if Wendy had a half-sister, which I get. But if it turns out that she does, how are you going to handle that? Do you imagine you and Carla and your kids could become one big happy family?"

I carried my tea into the living room and sat down. "I don't know. I'm still really angry with Alex. Though I'm trying to be level-headed about all this, I'm only human, and whenever I think about this woman with my husband, most of me wants to scratch her eyes out."

David chuckled. "I'm glad to hear it. I was starting to think you were superhuman, and that's intimidating."

I blew gently on my tea. "Nope. Not superhuman. Not by a long shot." David stayed on the phone with me while I picked up the remote control and turned on the TV.

"What I really want to know," I said, setting the remote down on the sofa cushion beside me, "are all the trashy details, like how long was the affair going on, and how did they meet? Was it a one-night stand and did she become like Glenn Close in *Fatal Attraction*? Or was he actually in love with her? Was he planning to leave Wendy and me?"

Just then, the computer chimed, alerting me that an email had come in.

"Oh…I just got an email." I rose quickly from the sofa and went to check it out. "Please don't let it be spam…"

I wiggled the mouse to turn on the screen light, and there it was—a personal reply from Carla Matthews.

"Oh my God," I said. "It's from *her*."

"What does it say?" David asked. "Can you read it to me?"

"Yes." I sat down with my tea. "Are you ready? Here goes…"

⸙

Dear Audrey,

I was surprised to get your email, as I'm not sure how you found me. Alex made me promise not to contact you or any member of his family—though I believe he would have told you about me eventually—but when he died, I couldn't bring myself to betray that request.

I was devastated when he was taken from us, as I'm sure you were as well, but it was very difficult for me because there was no one I could talk to about it. No one who actually knew him. None of my friends or family had ever met him.

I did attend his funeral, but I remained respectfully at the back of the church. I saw you and your daughter Wendy and I wished there was a way I could take away your pain. He was such a good man—the very best. Please accept my condolences for your loss.

I'm not sure where to go from here. Now that you've found me—and I'm so glad you did—it seems pointless to avoid meeting each other. We may have some difficult decisions to make about the future and whether or not to introduce my daughter Kaleigh to Alex's family. Maybe we could talk about that.

If you would like to come here to see me, we could meet at my place. The address is below. Any day this week would be fine. I work most evenings, so if you are free in the day, *that would be great. Let me know, and please bring your daughter. Alex told me so much about her. I would love to meet her!*

    Warmly,

    Carla

"Good Lord!" I said, sitting back in my chair. "Is that not weird? She has no shame. She makes no apologies."

"It is weird," David agreed. "Are you sure you want to get involved with her? What if she turns out to be like Melanie? What if she wants to latch on to you and Alex's family?"

I covered my cheeks with my hands. "What is that old saying? Let sleeping dogs lie? Maybe I should have just left it alone. What was I thinking? After getting my house burned down once, you'd think I would have learned my lesson."

"Hang on," David said. "At least you'll get answers when you meet her, because she certainly seems willing to be open about everything. And if you don't want to have any further contact with her afterward, you can make that clear. She's respected Alex's wishes for the past two years. That's a good sign."

"Yeah. But she came to his funeral," I mentioned. "She was there in the back of the church watching Wendy and me. That kind of creeps me out."

"Well, you can't fault her for attending," David said, gently reminding me to be sensible. "Obviously she cared for Alex, and at least she sat at the back. She didn't try to horn in. That tells us she has some degree of self-restraint."

"Maybe you're right," I replied. "But I don't know about bringing Wendy. I think I need to check her out first, make sure she's not Glenn Close."

David laughed. "Now, now. Glenn Close is supposedly a lovely woman in real life. But yes, it would be wise to do a recon mission first. And you shouldn't go alone. I'll come with you."

A large amount of tension drained out of me and I felt my shoulders relax. "I'd appreciate that, if you don't mind."

"Are you kidding me?" he replied. "I insist. Actually, I'm as curious as you are. I want to know the whole story."

"Me, too." I sat for a moment, taking it all in. "I'll email her back right now. Can you tell me what days you're free this week? Let's hope our schedules match up."

"I'll do whatever it takes," he replied, "so let's start with *your* schedule."

I felt slightly breathless. "You're awesome, you know."

He chuckled. "Flattery will get you everywhere."

J ean and Garry were wonderful, as always, about taking
Wendy for the day on Thursday—and not asking questions
about what I had planned—which allowed David and me to
travel to Boston together alone.

He had GPS in his vehicle, so we found Carla's apartment
building without any trouble, but when we pulled over at the curb
and he turned off the engine, I found myself glued to the seat.

"My heart's pounding," I said. "This is worse than public speaking."

He reached for my hand, raised it to his lips and kept his eyes
fixed on mine as he kissed it. "Everything's going to be fine," he
said. "I'm here and I'm not going anywhere."

The butterflies in my belly fluttered around, and I wasn't
sure if it was the touch of David's lips or the situation as a whole
that caused such a response in me. Either way, I was grateful to be
with him now, when I so desperately needed a friend.

"What would I have done without you these past few weeks?"
I asked, turning in my seat to face him. "You've been my rock."

"And you've amazed me at every turn," he replied. "Alex was
a lucky man."

Something intense flared through my veins and I knew in
that instant that my feelings for David were moving quickly and
steadily beyond mere friendship.

I couldn't think about that now, however. I needed to stay focused on getting the answers I needed about my marriage.

"You say he was a lucky man," I replied, "and yet…"

David laid a hand on my cheek. "If he cheated on you, it was *his* shortcoming, not yours. Don't ever let yourself think otherwise."

I nodded and finally felt ready to open the car door.

⸺⸺⸺

As we rode up ten floors in the elevator, all I could do was face forward in silence and watch the numbers blink on the display. Then *bing!* The doors slid open and it was time to step off.

I felt David's hand on the small of my back, guiding me as we walked the length of the narrow carpeted hall.

"Here it is," David said. "Are you ready?"

I nodded and he knocked on the door.

It swung open immediately, and there stood Carla, as if she had been listening for our footsteps all the way from the elevator.

She was strikingly beautiful with a tall, slim figure, clear skin, full lips, big brown eyes, and wavy honey-colored hair. I found myself staring at her in a foggy haze of disbelief.

Had this woman made love to my husband? Did she flirt with him and lure him away from his family? Did she not see the wedding ring? Was he even wearing it at their first meeting?

Anger welled up inside me, but I pushed it back down.

"Hi," she said, holding out her hand. "I'm Carla. You must be Audrey."

Then the most extraordinary thing happened. Her daughter—who looked to be about two years old—came barreling through to greet us with a smile.

"And this is Kaleigh," Carla said.

As soon as I saw the child, I knew that she belonged to Alex. She had the same dark features and charismatic eyes. The realization knocked me off balance emotionally, and I was confused by my feelings.

Part of me wanted to scoop the child up into my arms and hug her tight.

Another part of me wanted to shake the daylights out of Alex. If only I could.

Carla swept her daughter close, up against her leg. Her smile was radiant and I was briefly mesmerized. This reaction was immediately followed by bitter, sour-tasting jealousy.

"This is my friend David," I said, gesturing toward him.

"Oh yes." Carla shook his hand as well. "Alex spoke highly of you. He showed me pictures and told me about your work, and how you were friends since high school."

"It's nice to meet you," David said, and I suddenly found myself wishing I hadn't brought him after all, because I half expected Carla to flirt with him, too.

She stepped aside to make room for us to enter. "Come on in."

The layout of the place was standard for a high-rise apartment. The entry hall was narrow. There was a small kitchen to the left which opened to a modest-sized carpeted living room beyond.

David and I followed Carla and Kaleigh into the living room where she had a vegetable tray set out on the coffee table with a bowl of dip.

"Can I get you anything to drink?" she asked. "I have juice, pop and coffee. Or would you like a beer, David?"

"Nothing for me, thanks," I replied because I had no appetite.

THE COLOR OF A MEMORY

David, however, said he'd love a glass of water.

While Carla went to fill it at the sink in the kitchen, he and I sat down on the sofa and exchanged glances. He gave my hand a squeeze.

Carla returned and set his water on the coffee table. "There you go." Then she met my gaze as she took a seat in a facing chair. "I can't believe I'm finally meeting you. I've wanted to talk to you for so long. It was hard not to contact you over the past two years, but I always forced myself to resist. I didn't want to break my promise to Alex, but maybe he would have wanted me to.... I'm still not sure, but the fact that you found me makes me wonder if he *did* want that. Who knows?"

I swallowed over my disbelief. *Was this really happening?*

Little Kaleigh climbed up onto the sofa beside me and smiled. "You have pretty glasses," she said.

I smiled in return. "Thank you."

"She has a thing for the type of glasses you're wearing," Carla explained. "I don't know why. Maybe she saw something on TV."

Kaleigh continued to smile at me, and I was overcome by a perplexing mixture of emotions. She was an adorable little girl, and her eyes...They had the same spark as Alex's. It was the same spark that had made me fall in love with him.

Which made me feel hurt and betrayed.

Shifting uneasily in my seat, I tried to focus on all the questions I wanted to ask. "So how did you meet Alex?"

Carla stared at me for a moment, as if confused. "Well...I can't really remember the first time, I was too young...but in a way, I guess I've known him all my life."

I didn't know how to take that. Had they gone to kindergarten together or something?

She inclined her head at me. "You do know who I am, right?"

To her, I probably looked like a deer caught in the glare of car headlights as I shook my head, because I really knew nothing about this woman other than the fact that she worked as a waitress and had borne my husband's child.

Carla sat back in her chair and spoke bluntly, without hesitation. "I'm Alex's half-sister," she said. "We only found each other again the week before he died. Who did you *think* I was?"

The room spun in circles as I struggled to comprehend what she'd just told me.

Thank God David was sitting beside me, because I couldn't seem to make my mouth work.

"**Y**ou're Alex's *sister*?" David replied.

Carla nodded. "Half-sister. Oh, God, this is awkward. I'm not sure what's going on here. I thought you knew that."

David and I looked at each other. "We had no idea," he said. "Audrey found Kaleigh's ultrasound photo in Alex's car, and she assumed..." He stopped at that.

Carla's eyebrows lifted. "Oh my. Did you think I was having an affair with him? No, that's not it at all. Oh, Audrey..."

I covered my mouth with a hand. "I'm so sorry. I feel like an idiot."

She stared at me. "What made you think that?"

How could I ever explain? How could I tell her that I had lost faith in my husband, and that as soon as the first opportunity arose to confirm my early doubts about him...it was enough to convince me he was a cheater?

I felt ashamed, yet I understood why I wanted to believe this. Perhaps I needed a place to project my anger over losing him. Maybe a part of me felt it would be easier to believe he'd betrayed me—and to hate him—than to accept that I had lost such a perfect, wonderful man.

"Everything pointed to that," I told her, because it was true. The evidence had been compelling. "Just before he died he became withdrawn and I sensed something was off, and then when I found the picture in the car…Do you remember what you wrote on the back of it?"

Carla shook her head.

"You wrote: 'I hope she has your good looks.' And you drew a heart by your initial. Then we found an email from you that made it seem like he was going to leave us for you. It never occurred to me that it could be something else." I looked down at Kaleigh who was now playing behind a pink-and-white dollhouse under the window. "So she's Alex's niece?"

"That's right," Carla replied. "Half-niece."

Quietly I whispered, "Can I ask who her father is?"

Carla also spoke in hushed tones. "That's not a good story. He's someone I dated briefly a while back. I was in love with him, but he walked out on me when he found out I was pregnant. He left town—quite some time ago—and I haven't heard a word from him since. I was pregnant out to here when I reconnected with Alex." She gestured with her arms, as if she were holding a basketball in front of her tummy.

"I don't understand," I said. "Alex never mentioned a sister other than Sarah."

"That's because he didn't remember me," she explained, "nor did I remember him—and this is the part he wanted to keep secret, because he wanted to protect his mom. She never knew her husband was seeing someone else. So there *was* an affair going on. It just wasn't Alex, and it was many, many years ago."

I cupped my forehead in a hand. "I can't believe it."

I was both relieved and saddened to learn that it was Jean's husband who had been unfaithful. Alex had told me many times how deeply his mother loved his father and how long it had taken her to overcome the grief of losing him.

"Alex and I were born about a year apart," Carla explained, "and our father used to spend time with us together on Saturdays when we were both really young. That's how I found Alex two years ago. I kept having these vague, foggy memories of riding in an antique car and going to the race track with a boy I believed was my brother. My mom died in a car crash when I was five and I was sent to live with my aunt in Pennsylvania. That's when our father died, sometime after that, which is why I lost all contact with Alex. I was too young to investigate anything, and my aunt just swept everything under the rug, so to speak. So I just kind of buried it and went on about my life until recently, when I got pregnant. That's when I started having the dreams about that old car, driving around in the back seat and eating ice cream. I couldn't get the memories out of my head, so I went online looking for vintage cars and found a picture of one that looked exactly like what I remembered. It had a red pinstriped interior and a crystal knob on the gear shift at the steering wheel. I went into every chat room I could find and asked if anyone remembered going to the race track as a kid in an old Buick Street Rod."

"And Alex replied," I said.

Carla nodded. "He was just as confused as I was about those memories, because the way he remembered it, he thought he had gone to the track with his sister Sarah, but then he realized that she would have just been a baby then. He said he never really questioned it. He just thought his memory of it was hazy."

I recalled the day Alex and I sat in the Buick in his garage and he told me about those fond memories of his father taking him and his sister to the race track. I realized I hadn't done the math either, because he'd told me his father died when he was seven, yet Sarah would have been only about six months old. I remember Alex telling me how he and his sister would run to the creek to catch frogs.

"I don't understand why he wanted to keep this a secret," I said to Carla. "Why didn't he tell me?"

This was perhaps the most hurtful thing. *Did he not trust me? Did he feel it would reflect badly on him if I learned that his father had been unfaithful?*

Carla rested her temple on a finger. "He was shocked to learn about his father's affair, and he told me he needed time to figure out how to tell you and his mom. Actually, he was reluctant to *ever* tell his mother about it because he didn't want to spoil her perfect memory of him."

As I listened to all of this, my heart broke at the thought that Alex died without resolving this situation.

"Oh, Alex," I whispered, bowing my head with regret for all my suspicions and feelings of anger over the past few weeks. *How could I not have known? How could I not have trusted him to be the good husband and father he was—right up until the day he died?* He had never cheated. He didn't deserve my censure.

Maybe that's why he always had his back turned to me in my dreams. It was *me* who couldn't see him for the true and honorable man that he was.

David touched my shoulder. "Now you know," he softly said.

Needing to be held, I turned into his loving embrace.

"Now the burning question is this…" I said to David as we drove home from Boston that evening. "Do I, or do I not, tell Jean?"

David turned off the radio. "That's a tough one. I've known Jean since I was in high school and there was always a sense that she never got over losing Alex's dad. Their house was like a shrine with family pictures everywhere. I swear we all thought he was some sort of saint. But I remember Alex saying once that he wished his mom could move on, but it was like…a part of her had died, too."

"It certainly took her a long time to find someone," I replied. "I'm just glad she's happy now."

"Me, too. Garry's a good guy." David's eyes met mine and I saw a hint of melancholy in them. "What about *you*, Audrey? Now that you know Alex wasn't unfaithful, will you go on mourning, like Jean did?"

I gazed out the window at the passing landscape and thought about the relief—and love—I'd felt in Carla's apartment when I learned that Alex hadn't been unfaithful to me, and that he'd struggled with the decision to tell me about his father's infidelity because he was ashamed of it.

How easy it would be to idolize and cling to the memory of that integrity…

I looked at David, whose gaze was fixed on the road ahead of us. Then I touched his arm and asked, "Do you remember when you showed me the email from Carla, and I said it felt like Alex died all over again?"

David nodded.

"I honestly did feel that way," I continued, "and it brought everything back—the terrible heartache. Then today, when Carla told us she was his half-sister, I was ashamed of myself for doubting him, and all the love I felt for him came flooding back. It was as if he'd risen from the dead."

David took his eyes off the road for a few seconds to study my expression.

"But all that joy came from my *memory* of him," I explained. "I'm so glad now that it's not tarnished, that he really was the best husband and father in the world, and I can talk about him to Wendy without trying to hide any bitterness. I know now that I was right to trust my instincts and marry him, and that I can do that again…I can take a leap of faith—because the greatest joy I ever had was with Alex. I want to love like that again."

I noticed David's Adam's apple bob; a muscle twitched at his jaw. Then he checked the rearview mirror, flicked the blinker and pulled over, nearly skidding onto the side of the road.

My upper body jerked forward at the abrupt stop. David shifted the gears into park, leaned across the seat and pressed his mouth to mine with a passion that knocked me senseless and sent my head into a dizzying spin. I parted my lips and opened myself to a violent rush of emotion.

He kissed me hard until the luscious damp pressure of his mouth caused a tingle of excitement in all the outer reaches of my body.

My skin erupted in goose bumps, and when he drew back, I felt shaky all over. I was completely overwhelmed.

"I can love you like that," he said in a low, husky voice that caused my body to melt like butter. "I've loved you since the first day I saw you in the ER, and God, there were moments I hated Alex for being the one who broke his foot that day. I wanted it to be me."

My breath caught in my throat and my eyebrows lifted. "I didn't know."

"Well, now you do," he replied with a flirtatious glimmer in his eye that made me weak in the knees. Thank God I was sitting down.

He kissed me again, then resumed his position in the driver's seat and shifted back into first gear.

"Let's go home then," he said with a manly confidence that turned every inch of my quivering body into a pile of sticky jelly, "and figure out where to go from here—and what in the world we're going to tell Jean."

After a great deal more discussion, David helped me decide how to handle the Carla and Kaleigh situation with Jean, but first I needed to call Nadia and tell her the latest developments, because she'd been instrumental in helping me locate Carla.

As I dialed Nadia's number, I experienced a strange sensation of excitement, as if by telling her about my incredible day, I was also telling Alex, somehow by proxy. I knew that was crazy, but oh, how I wanted him to know that I'd found his half-sister. I also wanted him to know that I intended to make her a part of my life and Wendy's.

Without a shadow of a doubt, I knew he would be pleased to hear it.

If only he could have known before he passed.

Nadia's phone rang three times before she picked up. "Hello?"

"Hi Nadia. It's Audrey."

She greeted me warmly and asked how the day had gone. "Did you meet her?"

"Yes," I told her, "and it turned out totally different from what I expected. You're not going to believe this."

Nadia was quick to reply. "Tell me."

I paused—just for dramatic effect. "Carla Matthews was Alex's *half-sister.*"

The news was met with silence, then Nadia exhaled. "Wow. He never told you about her?"

"He didn't even know," I explained. "Not until the week before he died. He did once tell me about his vague memories of going to the race track in the Buick with his sister when he was really young, but he thought it was Sarah. Turns out it wasn't. It was Carla."

The clock ticked ominously on the wall beside me.

"Does that mean his father cheated on Jean?" Nadia asked.

I sank onto one of the kitchen chairs. "Yes, and that's the difficult part. It's why Alex was so secretive. He didn't want his mom to know about Carla. He was very protective of her. He was a good man, Nadia. The very best. Remember when I told you in the playground that he had a good heart? He *did.* There can be no doubt about that now."

I heard the smile in Nadia's voice. "I'm so happy to hear it. I'm happy for both of us."

"Me, too. On that note, can I ask you a question?"

"Sure."

"Would you like to meet Carla? Because if you want to, when we come to your place Saturday, we could bring her and Kaleigh. I know she'd love to meet *you.*"

Nadia didn't hesitate. "That's a great idea. Our three girls will have a blast on the new play structure. But there's only one problem."

"What's that?" I asked.

"I've already invited Jean," Nadia replied, "so things could get awkward."

I stood up to make some tea. "Yes, they could. I guess I need to give her a call."

"What will you tell her?" Nadia asked.

I wished I could answer the question, but I still wasn't sure if it was the right thing to do. Jean's husband's affair was in the past now. He'd been dead for years. Was she better off not knowing? Or was it more important that she have some contact with her late son's niece and half-sister?

Most importantly, what would Alex have wanted?

"I'm not sure yet," I replied, "but I'll let you know before Saturday.

We hung up so I could dial Jean's number.

CHAPTER

Fifty-two

The following morning, I pulled into Jean's driveway and turned off the car.

David wasn't scheduled to work that day so he volunteered to watch Wendy so I could have some time alone with Jean.

"Come on in," she said cheerfully as she opened the door. "I just made us some carrot muffins."

"*Mmm,* they smell delicious," I replied as I crossed the threshold and followed her to the kitchen.

Planting myself at the breakfast bar, I reveled in the aroma of hot muffins straight out of the oven. Jean set a plate in front of me and slid the butter dish closer. "Coffee?"

"I'd love some," I replied as I reached for a warm muffin and peeled back the paper.

A moment later we were both seated. She gently asked how I was getting along—as if *I* was the one who needed help and comfort. I regretted that it wouldn't be long before the shoe would be on the other foot.

"Actually, there's something I want to talk to you about," I said. "It's about Alex, sort of."

Her expression clouded over with concern. "What is it, Audrey?"

I had thought long and hard about this decision—whether or not to tell Jean about Carla and Kaleigh—and it was vitally important to me that I respect Alex's wishes. But now that he was gone, how could I know—how could *anyone* know—what he truly would have wanted?

In the end, I chose to follow to my heart, to trust that I knew the man he was deep down—just like I did on the bridge that day when he dropped to one knee before me and proposed. I'd said yes because I loved him and I believed we were meant to be together, and it turned out I was right to put all my faith in him. Now it was time to put my faith in my own heart and intuition.

Setting down my butter knife, I leaned back on the white leather stool. "It's something I've been keeping from you for a little while, and I'm sorry about that. It started a few weeks ago when I was here for the two-year anniversary of Alex's death. Remember when I went out to sit in the Buick and didn't come back for a long time? Then I left abruptly?"

"Of course I remember."

I dropped my gaze to the granite countertop of the breakfast bar and blinked a few times, fighting to gather the right words.

"I found something in the glove box of the car that day. It was an ultrasound of a baby, and there was a note to Alex on the back that suggested the child belonged to him. Ever since then, I thought maybe he'd been having an affair before he died, but it turns out he wasn't."

Jean blinked a few times, then sat back in shock. "Well, thank God for that."

I nodded. "I agree. I was relieved to find out he wasn't cheating on me...but that's where it gets complicated." I paused for a moment, then met her gaze directly. "The woman who was pregnant—the one who'd had the ultrasound…She was *related* to Alex."

I stopped before going any further because I couldn't bring myself to be blunt. I didn't want to hurt Jean. I had no idea how to tell her the truth, but I knew I had to.

She stared at me intently. "How do you mean…*related*?"

I breathed deeply and let it out. "The woman was his half-sister."

While I gave Jean a few seconds to make sense of what I was trying to tell her, I began to perspire heavily. I shrugged out of my sweater and let it drape on the back of the chair, then wiped my forehead with the back of a hand.

"Was her name Carla?" Jean asked.

My lips parted in surprise. "Yes. It was." I felt my eyebrows pull together in dismay. "Did you know about her?"

Jean slowly nodded. "I certainly knew who her mother was. William tried to keep it from me, of course, but I knew. A wife always knows."

"But you forgave him?"

Her hesitation surprised me, and she shrugged. "Not really, but I did my best to keep everything together. For Alex and Sarah."

A puff of air sailed out of my lungs. "But everyone thought you *worshipped* Alex's father. Alex thought that was the reason you didn't remarry for such a long time…Because you couldn't get over the loss of him."

Jean shook her head. "What I couldn't get over was my anger at his infidelity. To put it simply, I didn't *want* to get married again because I didn't feel I could ever trust another man. But then Garry came along and he changed my mind."

The timer on the microwave beeped, and Jean got up to turn it off. "I set that to remind me to put some meat in the slow cooker for dinner," she told me. Then she moved to open the fridge.

I watched her withdraw a package of chicken, set it on the counter and remove the cellophane wrap.

"You don't seem upset," I said.

She shook her head, but didn't meet my gaze. "I'm over the fact that William cheated. I've been over it for a long time, but I always regretted that Alex didn't get to know his half-sister better. All my life I've felt guilty about that, but I didn't know how to change it. I didn't know much about the girl except what Alex told me when he was little, after William brought him home from the race track on Saturdays. At first I thought Carla was Alex's imaginary friend, but eventually I figured out that she must be the daughter of the woman William was seeing. I knew he loved her and I think he might have left me for her eventually, if he hadn't passed away."

Jean dropped the meat into the slow cooker and threw the Styrofoam packaging into the garbage. She then returned to the stool and sat down, but stared off into space for a while.

"Are you okay?" I asked.

She met my gaze at last. "Did you say there was an ultrasound photo?"

Gathering my composure, I reached into my purse, dug it out and handed it to her. "Here it is."

She examined it closely, then turned it over to read the hand-written note on the back. Finally, her hand flew to her mouth. She broke down and wept.

I stood up to wrap my arms around her. I didn't know what to say.

When at last she collected herself, she handed the picture back to me and wiped the tears from her cheeks. "Alex would have been this baby's uncle?"

I nodded. "I went to visit Carla yesterday and I met Kaleigh, her daughter. She's two years old now and she looks a lot like Alex."

Jean wiped her eyes again and chuckled with a hint of bitterness. "Then she must look like William, too, because that's where Alex got all his charm."

"I see," I replied, pleased at least that the worst shock of this was over—and to know that Alex may have inherited his father's good looks, but somehow he'd learned something along the way and hadn't repeated his father's indiscretions.

Jean and I sat for a moment, contemplating the situation.

"Was I right to tell you?" I asked her. "I struggled with it. I thought maybe you'd be better off not knowing."

Her eyes lifted. "God, no. I've been wondering about little Carla for years. Now that I know she's out there—that you found her and she has a daughter—I feel as if there might be some hope that I can make amends for not telling Alex when he was alive. How is she? Do you think she'd want to meet us? Because if she's connected to my son by blood, I can't imagine not knowing her. Enough time has passed. My anger toward William is gone now. I just want to know that Carla is okay, and I want her to know that she has family. I'm certain it's what Alex would have wanted."

I covered Jean's hand with my own. "I believe you're right about that, and I think maybe he was the one who led us to her." I touched my forehead to hers and smiled. "Maybe he called to us both from the Buick."

Fifty-three

The sun rose high and bright in the sky on the day of Nadia's barbeque in Waltham. David and I pulled into the driveway with Carla, Kaleigh and Wendy in the back seat of his Hyundai Tucson. We all spilled out laughing when the girls couldn't contain themselves at the sight of Nadia's new play structure. It boasted a two-level clubhouse with French windows, a spiral wave slide, two swings and a glider, a rock climbing wall, monkey rings and a water cannon.

"Let the fun begin," David said as he stepped out and looked around the lush green yard.

Nadia and Jesse came out to greet us, and Ellen led our girls to the swing set.

"You must be Carla," Nadia said. She introduced Jesse and invited us all to sit on the porch where we could watch the girls play.

Since David was driving, Carla and I opted for chilled wine with raspberries, and it wasn't long before we were laughing and sharing parenting tips and tales about our girls.

Eventually, Carla broached the subject of our connection as a group, and she leaned forward in her deck chair to address Nadia.

"How has your health been since the transplant?" she asked. "I read up on organ donation, and it's quite a fascinating subject."

"Fascinating and miraculous," Nadia replied. "I wouldn't be alive today if it wasn't for your brother's generous gift." She laid a hand over her heart. "I feel him in here every day, and I'm so grateful for the choice he and his family made."

Another vehicle pulled into the driveway just then, and Jesse rose to his feet. "It's Jean and Garry." He ventured down the stairs to greet them.

Carla and I shared a look. We had talked about everything in great depth, and I knew she was uneasy about meeting Jean.

We waited patiently on the covered veranda while Jesse met them in the driveway, chatted for a few minutes, then escorted them up the stairs.

"This is Jean and Garry," Jesse said. "Of course they know most of us, but this is Carla, and that's Carla's daughter Kaleigh on the swing set."

Carla stood up and held out her hand. "It's nice to meet you."

Jean smiled warmly. "And it's about time, don't you think?"

Instead of shaking Carla's hand, she stepped forward and pulled her into her arms.

I was pleased to see the ice broken, then we all settled in for the afternoon to get to know each other better.

A few days after the barbeque at Nadia's home in Waltham, I sat bolt upright in bed, waking from a dream that left me gasping for air.

Not because I was fearful or panicked, but because I was exultant.

In the dream, I was strolling down a sandy beach with Alex. We were holding hands and the setting sun sparkled like starlight off the water as foamy waves rolled onto the beach in a smooth, steady rhythm. I felt deeply loved, and I laughed when Alex suggested we take off our clothes and go for a swim.

"It's too cold," I replied with a laugh as I ran ahead of him.

He proceeded to remove his shirt, then he kicked off his shoes and dropped his pants.

"You're crazy!" I shouted, watching him dash into the waves, naked as the day he was born. He dove in, then broke the surface and waved at me.

I waved back at him, then he turned and swam in the other direction, out to sea.

For a long time I stood on the beach, shading my eyes with a hand until he was a tiny speck in the distance.

That's when I woke up…feeling joyful.

❦

One Year Later

On the third anniversary of Alex's death, Jean suggested that David and I take the Buick out for a spin.

We'd just enjoyed an afternoon of good food and fine wine, which she and Garry served on their back patio where the hummingbirds were flitting about in record numbers.

She invited Nadia, Jessie and Ellen, Carla and Kaleigh, David, Wendy and me.

David and I had been seeing each other exclusively and devotedly since the day we kissed on the side of the road after meeting Carla. We were now engaged and planning a traditional church wedding—something I'd missed out on when I married Alex in such a hurry years ago. I had no regrets about that—because I've come to realize every moment is precious and none should be squandered—but I was excited about having the time to choose a wedding dress and a cake and plan an extravagant honeymoon that would last longer than three days.

David and I planned to fly to New Zealand for two weeks in October, rent a car and see as much of the country as we could. Jean had volunteered to take care of Wendy, but she fully expected us to come home with the beginnings of another grandchild for her to spoil.

But first, tonight, we had to take the Buick out for a spin and pay homage to Alex and his love for old cars and classic tunes on the radio.

Wendy, Kaleigh and Ellen begged to come along, so we buckled them into booster seats in the back, rolled down the windows and drove off in search of ice cream with sprinkles.

"Whose car is this?" Wendy shouted giddily. "Is it Grandpa Garry's?"

"You know whose car it is," I replied with a teasing grin, turning to look over my shoulder.

"It's Daddy's," she said.

"That's right. And Wendy's daddy is your Uncle Alex," I said to Kaleigh, who nodded at me. "And who is he to you?" I asked Ellen, who was seated in the middle.

"He gave his heart to my Mom," she replied.

"Very good," I replied, pleased they all knew that this car had once belonged to an incredible man.

"When are we going to get ice cream?" Wendy asked.

David pointed at the shop just ahead. "In about two minutes," he replied. "Do you think you can wait that long?"

"No!" they all shrieked simultaneously.

David and I laughed and clasped hands on the seat, then I turned up the radio so we could all sing along with Elvis.

Epilogue

What a life I've lived, but it's not over yet. There are still so many joys left to celebrate.

How blessed I feel to be able to look back on my years so far and know that my life has been splendid and magical, and all my experiences—even the painful things—were meant to unfold exactly as they did.

I wouldn't trade any of it for the world, not even the hardships. No matter how difficult it was to lose Alex, I would never wish to erase the time we had together and the daughter we created. My goal now is to be strong and continue to heal…to keep living, learning, and loving. To have faith in the future and myself.

I still miss Alex every day, but I know he's in a good place now, watching over all of us, perhaps coming to visit us in our dreams.

That's the beauty of a memory, isn't it? It's the place in our hearts where we can hold onto our loved ones forever.

Rest in peace, Alex Fitzgerald. Perhaps we will all be together again someday.

For more information about this book and others in the Color of Heaven series, please visit the author's website at www.juliannemaclean.com. While you're there, be sure to sign up for Julianne's newsletter to stay informed about upcoming releases as they are announced.

Read on for an excerpt from

The COLOR
of
LOVE

book six in the Color of Heaven series.

Prologue

How powerful is love, exactly? Is it strong enough to ward off death? And if so, where does that sort of warrior love come from? Who creates it or sends it to you when you're shivering in a cold dark cave, alone and without hope? Is it God? Or are we, each of us, on our own, responsible for the love that grows and lives in our hearts?

By all accounts, I should be a dead man. It's a miracle I'm alive today to tell this story, which brings me back to my initial question: Does love have the power to thrust a person into danger, test his fortitude, push him to the brink of madness, all for the sole purpose of leading him to the place he's meant to be? Or is it all just luck and coincidence?

I still don't know the answers to those questions, and I have no idea why certain events in my life transpired as they did. All I know is that the result was extraordinary and astounds me to this day.

What is so special about me? Who am I?

I am just a man—a man who was saved by love.

Choices

CHAPTER

One

Adapted from the journal of Seth Jameson

I'm not sure where to begin, so I guess I'll start by thanking God that I brought this empty notebook on the plane. I'm not much of a writer but clearly there's a story here to tell, so I'll do my best to document everything that has happened so far.

I only hope I don't run out of paper or ink before we're rescued.

If we're rescued.

It's been four days and we haven't seen a single sign of anything resembling a search.

But let me go back first, and explain how I got here.

It all began two weeks ago when I received a phone call from Mike Lawson, one of my climbing buddies from Australia. Mike and I had grown up together and we met in Nepal fifteen years ago on our first Everest expedition, and reached the summit together in a perfect moment of triumph and exhaustion.

I was only twenty-one at the time (Mike was twenty-four) and I've since reached the summit six times. Not on my own, of course. I've been working as a team leader and guide, helping others travel up the mountain from base camp to achieve their dreams. Mike has remained a close friend and twice he has joined me to help guide others to the top of the world.

Outside of that, we spend a good deal of time apart, pursuing our own personal ambitions, climbing mountains all over the world and always seeking out media opportunities that could lead to sponsorships, with the goal to find a way to feed our alpine addictions.

As I write these words—while contemplating the unbelievable situation I find myself in—I can't possibly deny the truth of that statement. That my desire to scale mountains is exactly that: an addiction I have never been able to control.

Just like alcohol or cocaine, the craving to propel myself to new and different peaks each year holds me in its grip, causing me to ignore and lose sight of the people who matter most in my life, while I selfishly feed the beast inside me.

Two weeks ago, Mike called me at my cabin in Maine to discuss a mountaineering prospect in Iceland. Because we keep in touch regularly through social media, I already knew Mike had been hired by George Atherton, a billionaire philanthropist, to lead a group of climbers to the top of the Eyjafjallajökull volcano.

It's an easy one-day hike over snow and ice, but what interested me most about the expedition was the fact that a camera crew would be tagging along to film a documentary about the billionaire who was funding the trip.

Mike had intended to lead the hike with his current climbing partner and significant other, Julie Peters, but Julie broke her ankle while skiing in Quebec a week before shooting was scheduled to begin. Mike wanted me to drop everything and fly to Iceland to take her place.

Since I'd been dealing with my Everest clients through email (that expedition will occur in March, April and May), I didn't see why I couldn't continue to manage that from Iceland and make a few extra bucks in the process. The film shoot was supposed to be a quick three-day gig, after all, and who knew what might come of it? Mike and I both want to make names for ourselves in the climbing world, and judging by the filmmakers who are on board for the project, it's quite possible that the doc could win some awards.

Naturally, I said yes and hopped a flight to Halifax, Nova Scotia, where I connected with some members of the film crew. We then flew directly to Reykjavik on Mr. Atherton's private corporate jet.

It was a decision I now wish I could reverse.

Everything seemed normal during takeoff. Though perhaps "normal" isn't the right word to describe the flight, for there I sat—Mr. Cheapskate Economy Class—in a soft and spacious mocha-colored swiveling leather chair. I was unshaven with a slouchy ribbed woolen toque on my head, my backpack at my feet, enjoying fifty-year-old single malt scotch on the rocks in a sparkling crystal tumbler. I don't want to overdo it, but just before takeoff, the producer handed me a box of assorted Swiss chocolates. I opened it and helped myself.

I'd never flown in such luxury before and couldn't believe my good luck. *How did I get here?* I wondered.

There were only three of us on board—not including the two pilots—but none of us had met before.

The guy beside me who'd handed me the chocolates was one of the producers of the documentary. His name was Jason Mehta and he told me he was nervous about the climb because he wasn't much of an outdoorsman. The most strenuous thing he ever did was run on a treadmill at the city gym.

I assured him he had nothing to worry about because it was more of a "hike" than an actual "climb."

(Secretly—because I'd already summited Everest five times— I felt it was beneath me to lead climbers on such an easy excursion, but I didn't express that to anyone, least of all Mike.)

The guy across from me in the facing seat was a cameraman, and he was mostly concerned about his equipment and how the batteries were going to hold up in the cold temperatures at high altitudes.

He told me his name was Aaron and he was from Boston.

"I'm Seth," I said, leaning forward to shake his hand. "Good to meet you."

He fell asleep not long after takeoff, so we didn't speak again until much later.

I still don't know what went wrong. Neither of us do. All we remember is waking up to some wicked turbulence somewhere over the Atlantic.

"What the hell?" I groaned, waking from a nap and sitting up in my seat to look out the window.

Beyond the glass, it was pitch black except for the flashing navigation lights on the wingtip of the aircraft, which sent an eerie glow into the clouds.

Bang! Crash! The plane thumped up and down.

I'd never experienced such a deafening clamor on a jet before, and it caused my insides to wrench into a tight knot. I gripped the armrests with both hands and met Aaron's gaze across from me. He must have woken up around the same time I did.

"Geez," he said, his body pressed stiffly against the seat back. "They need to get us out of here."

"No kidding," Jason agreed.

Bump! Thwack! A warning bell pinged repeatedly.

The three of us fell silent while the plane shuddered and thrashed about in the sky, pitching and rolling in a sickening sequence of side-to-side figure eights.

At last the plane leveled out, but it continued to slam up and down on giant boulder-like pockets of air.

I'd never felt such fear. All I could do was clench my jaw, grip the armrests and squeeze my eyes shut while I prayed for everything to be over.

Then suddenly the nose of the plane dipped sharply and we plunged forward into a rapid, spiraling descent. Jason began screaming in terror, but I could utter no sounds. My chest and lungs constricted; my vocal chords wouldn't work.

My mind was screaming, however. Dreadful thoughts were banging around inside my head.

I didn't want to die. I wanted to live and fix the things I'd done wrong.

Please God, make it stop. I just want one more chance. If you let me live, I'll do better. I'll be a better father. I won't break any more promises.

But God couldn't have been listening, because we continued to dive toward the earth while the hellish terror raged on.

At no point did the pilots say anything to us on the intercom. Looking back on it, I suppose they were too busy fighting with the controls, trying to save our lives.

In those final moments, I opened my eyes and turned my head toward the window. There was nothing out there but blackness, interrupted only by the rapid flashing of the wing light on the mist.

⁕

As we were going down, I was certain we were all going to die. I believed it because I assumed we were crashing into the ice-filled waters of the North Atlantic.

I wish I could describe all the details of the crash, but it happened so fast I could barely make sense of it. All I remember is the motion of the plane as the engine roared, then the nose pointed upward ever so slightly, and I felt a strong, sudden lift beneath us, as if we were taking off again.

The sensation gave me hope. Was it possible the pilots had regained control? But the very next instant, we were jolted in our seats as the wing of the plane collided with something and broke away. The deafening sound of steel ripping apart and glass shattering overwhelmed my ability to think. Somehow, through my debilitating panic, I managed to turn my head and saw a gaping hole in the side the plane.

The seat Jason had occupied only seconds ago was gone and that part of the floor was missing.

A fierce ice-cold wind gusted through the interior of the cabin as we scraped at full speed over jagged treetops. Evergreen branches and trunks splintered and exploded as we careened through woods, and I felt as if my insides were going to burst into flame from the sheer fright of it all.

I don't know what finally stopped us. I must have blacked out for those final seconds because when I opened my eyes and sucked in a breath, everything was dark and quiet.

Was I blind? Or dead?

The whole world seemed to have gone pitch black. There were no cabin lights, no sounds of movement or voices.

Only then, when the freezing air entered my throat, did I know I was alive.

Feeling suddenly trapped, I thrashed about in my seat and struggled to unbuckle myself, but my hands shook uncontrollably. I could barely get a grip on anything.

When at last I was free, I leaned forward to squint through the darkness at Aaron, the cameraman from Boston, who was seated across from me. All I could decipher was the shadow of his immobile form. Was he alive? I had no idea.

"Aaron," I managed to mutter. "Are you all right?"

He gave no reply.

Then I remembered my cell phone in the pocket of my vest. I'd turned it off just before takeoff, but it was fully charged.

Quickly withdrawing it, I pushed the power button and waited for the screen to light up.

The familiar musical sound of the device filled me with relief, and I waited for it to find a signal so I could dial 911.

But there was no service. "Damn it," I whispered, then leaned forward in my seat to shine the glow of the screen upon Aaron.

He was hunched over sideways. His whole face was drenched in blood.

"Oh God," I whispered. Moving closer to try and help him, I took hold of his wrist and found a pulse, then shone my cell phone light over the top of his head to search for the source of the bleeding.

It appeared to be a clean gash just above his hairline, but not life threatening, as long as his skull wasn't fractured. He must have been sliced by a flying piece of metal or some other loose object.

"Aaron," I said, shaking his shoulder. "Can you hear me?"

Still, he offered no response, so I applied pressure to the wound for a moment while I tried to figure out what to do next.

Rising from my seat, I searched for my backpack and found it shoved up against the bulkhead. Quickly I rifled through it for my flashlight, knife, and first aid kit, then returned to help him.

Within minutes I had wrapped a bandage around his head and was on my feet, checking my cell phone for service again.

Still nothing, and I'd spent enough time in remote locations to know that if I let the phone continue to search for a signal, the battery would be dead within an hour. So I shut it down to conserve the battery, slipped it into my back pocket and shone my flashlight around what was left of the interior of the plane.

For a somber moment, I paused to stare at the place where Jason had been sitting not long ago. How lucky for me that I had chosen my seat and not his when we boarded.

Poor Jason. I wondered if he was alive out there somewhere…

Beneath the hole in the floor was a bed of snow, and along the open side, a thick wall of evergreen boughs.

Carefully, I turned and made my way toward the flight deck to check on the pilots.

To get there, I had to step over my large backpack and a mess of dented aluminum crates that must have flown forward from the galley.

I found the cockpit door unlocked, but I struggled to open it because the panel was warped and had become wedged against the floor.

When I finally squeezed through the narrow opening and shone my light on the scene, it was not what I'd hoped to find.

The nose section of the jet had been completely smashed in. Thick spruce branches filled what was left of the space. I wrestled with the prickly growth, fighting to thrust the disorderly green boughs out of the way, but in the end, all I found were two dead pilots, their bodies crushed between the flight control panel and bulkhead.

The gruesome sight of their lifeless eyes caused me to lose my breath, and I stumbled back, fell out of the cockpit and landed on my back on top of the cabin debris.

Panic and nausea flooded through me. I slammed the door shut with my boot.

That's when I heard the scream.

"It's okay, it's okay!" I shouted as I scrambled to my feet and hurried to Aaron's side.

He was thrashing about in his seat like a chained-up animal.

"We're okay!" I assured him. "The plane crashed, but we're fine."

He fumbled clumsily with the seatbelt buckle. "Get me out of here."

"It's easy. Look…There." I flicked the mechanism and freed him.

Aaron leapt out of his seat and tripped over my backpack.

"Where are we?" he asked, his eyes darting about.

"We're inside the plane," I explained. "We crashed into some trees, but I don't know anything more than that."

He took a moment to gather his wits. "Are we in Iceland?" he asked.

I was relieved that he was at least conscious of where we'd been heading. I was worried for a few seconds that because of his head wound he might not remember anything.

"I don't think so," I replied. "Based on when we left Halifax, we're probably in Newfoundland. I thought we were over the water when we were going down, but clearly we weren't, which was damn lucky for us. Or maybe it wasn't luck. Maybe the pilots had intentionally flown us to dry land."

Aaron wobbled and staggered sideways, then reached for the back of a seat to steady himself.

"Sit down." I reached out to help him. "You were hit on the head."

"Shit," he said.

"Don't worry. It's a clean wound and I stopped the bleeding, but you might have a mild concussion. I don't know. I'm not a doctor."

Aaron sat still for a moment, staring straight ahead. "Where's Jason?" he asked.

I hesitated, then shook my head. "The wing of the plane was ripped off when we were landing. He must have been sucked out. It's possible he might be alive somewhere, if we weren't too far off the ground when he fell. He was buckled into his seat, so the cushions might have provided some padding."

"Should we go look for him?" Aaron asked.

Again I shook my head. "It's too dark. We'll wait until morning, and even then, we shouldn't stray too far because the search planes will be looking for the wreckage. We'll need to be ready to signal them."

"You think they'll come in the morning?" Aaron asked.

"Of course, if not before then," I replied. "This jet belongs to a billionaire. I'm sure he'll be missing it, and the pilots must have radioed that we were in trouble."

Aaron slouched back in the seat and closed his eyes. "What about the pilots?"

"Both dead," I told him without elaborating. "And there's no power and the nose is completely crushed, so I don't think there's any hope of using the radio. I tried my cell phone but couldn't get a signal."

"What about GPS so we know where we are?"

I shook my head. "Without a mobile network, my phone will be dead within an hour just trying to find a signal. I'm keeping it shut off for now."

Neither of us said anything for a long time, then Aaron began to shiver. "It's freezing in here."

Maybe it was adrenaline, but I'd barely noticed the cold until he mentioned it. Then I realized my extremities were growing numb.

Geez. I was a seasoned climber and wasn't proud of the fact that I hadn't been more on top of this. I blamed it on the shock of the crash.

"You're right," I said. "We need to keep warm and make it through the night without freezing. That's the most important thing. Help me get some stuff out of my pack."

We barely slept a wink that night.

Because I had only one sleeping bag and we couldn't find Aaron's jacket (it must have blown out of the plane when the wing broke off, along with his cell phone which was in the pocket), we had to share what I had in my pack. This included an insulated parka I'd brought in addition to the jacket I was wearing.

We didn't talk much. What exactly do you chat about with a total stranger when you're shivering in the cold and weighing the fact that you just survived a plane crash, when others didn't? And two of those lost souls were only a few feet away, so it seemed proper, somehow, to remain silent.

When the sun finally came up, I nudged Aaron, tossed off the sleeping bag, and rose stiffly. My body felt sluggish and heavy from the cold, but my hands and feet were okay. I told Aaron to keep checking his extremities and not to ignore any numbness, then I crossed to the hole in the side of the plane to examine the situation in the light of day.

"We need to get out of here and see where we are," I said, "and make sure the wreckage is visible from the sky."

With the daylight, it was easier to establish what we were dealing with, at least in terms of an exit strategy. I made sure my gloves were on tight, then attempted to push some of the prickly branches out of the way. I discovered we were wedged tightly up against a giant black spruce.

"We won't be leaving through here," I said, giving up the task.

"Let's try the door," Aaron suggested.

Together we managed to open the passenger door which included an integral set of steps. I descended first and hopped into a foot and a half of snow.

"You stay where you are for now," I said to Aaron who stood on the steps. "It's important to stay dry."

There was not a single breath of wind in the air as I waded through the snow to gain some distance from the plane and get a better view of the wreckage.

"*Jesus...*" I whispered as I took in the devastated nose section and strips of steel ripped like thin ribbons from the length of the fuselage. The tail end was in shreds too. It was a miracle Aaron and I had survived.

"It doesn't help that the plane is white," I said to him. "The trees are tall and covered in snow. The branches are hiding most of the wreckage. Let's hope we left an obvious trail of damage when we were landing."

A snowflake fell on my nose just then. I looked up through a hole in the trees at the cloudy sky. *Great... Just what we need.*

"They should know where we are, though, shouldn't they?" Aaron asked. "I mean...the pilots must have radioed that we were in trouble."

"Of course," I replied, wading back to the plane. "But still, we should do something to make it easier for them to spot us. I have a red tent in my backpack. We'll find the nearest clearing and fly it like a flag. And we should keep busy today in case they don't find us right away. We'll need to light a fire to keep warm and then take stock of what we have for supplies."

I returned to the steps and glanced briefly at the pilots' frozen remains, visible through the smashed-in window as I climbed back up.

Again, I thought about what had been on my mind as the plane was zigzagging through the turbulence and I believed we were plunging to our deaths.

Carla and Kaleigh.

The snow began to fall lightly around 9:00 a.m., and by noon Aaron and I were huddled inside the plane, grateful to have a roof over our heads while a vicious blizzard raged outside.

I didn't bother to find a place to lay out my tent as a distress signal because it would have been buried within an hour. Either that, or it would have been ripped away by the wind.

And we couldn't venture out to search for Jason.

All we could do was sit and wait out the storm, uncomfortably aware that any potential search and rescue attempts would also have to be postponed until the weather cleared.

"I guess it's lucky for me that you're a mountaineer," Aaron said as he rubbed his palms together over the small fire I'd lit on an aluminum tray inside the plane. "I can honestly say, no one else I know would pull an ice ax, ropes and a thermal sleeping bag out of his carry-on."

I leaned back in my seat and regarded Aaron curiously. "I have two axes. One for each hand. But you must know something about climbing if they hired you to film us going up the side of the volcano."

He chuckled. "No, I'm a city boy through and through. This isn't even my day job. I'm just here because I own a decent high def camera and a Go Pro."

"You're kidding me." My eyebrows pulled together in surprise. "So you don't know anything about climbing?"

"Not a thing." He raised his boot to show me. "I just bought these hiking boots two days ago, and I got the Go Pro because I wanted to film tropical fish when I went snorkeling in Mexico last year."

"What's your day job, then?" I asked, intrigued but unimpressed.

"I'm a therapist, and I teach guitar lessons on the side."

"How do you know George Atherton?"

Aaron continued to hold his hands over the fire. "He's a client."

Maybe it was bad manners, but I laughed. "So are you his therapist or his guitar teacher?"

"Therapist. But don't worry, he hired an experienced D.O.P. to be in charge of the shoot, and from what I hear, the guy's a real pro." Aaron leaned to the side and gestured toward his camera case at the front of the plane. "I doubt I'll be shooting anything now. My camera's probably wrecked."

"Cameras can be replaced," I carefully reminded him.

Aaron's gaze met mine. "Yeah. We were lucky last night."

While we considered the loss of life and pondered the miracle of our existence on that day, the wind howled like a beast through the treetops overhead. Then suddenly...*boom*! There was a thunderous explosion and the whole plane shook.

Aaron jolted and looked up. "What was that?"

I remained seated in a lazy sprawl, slightly amused as I peered up at him. "Relax city boy. A big clump of snow just slid off a tree and landed on the roof."

He let out a breath and relaxed. "Ah." Then he frowned. "No chance we'll get buried alive in here…"

"Don't worry," I replied. "I'm keeping a close eye on the situation."

"Good to know," he said uneasily.

As I watched him lay another stick on the fire, I wondered if I should search for that bottle of single malt scotch, because the poor guy was seriously out of his element. He could probably have used a drink or two right then.

I could have used a couple myself.

News

Carla Matthews
Boston, Massachusetts

I was in the kitchen cooking cheesy bowtie pasta for Kaleigh when the telephone rang. She had just arrived home from school and was doing her homework on the sofa.

"Hello," I said, resting the receiver on my shoulder as I strained the pasta over the sink.

The voice on the other end caught me by surprise. I immediately set down the colander and turned to face Kaleigh, who was punching numbers into her calculator and scribbling in her notebook.

"Hi Gladys," I said. "It's nice to hear from you. It's been a while."

Over a year, in fact.

Not that I was counting the days or anything.

But *seriously*. One would think a sixty-year-old woman living alone would take more interest in seeing her only grandchild.

Like mother like son, I supposed.

"What's going on?" I asked.

She breathed heavily into the mouthpiece and let out a tiny whimper.

With growing concern, I faced the sink again. "What's wrong? Are you all right?"

"I'm fine," she replied at last, "but something's happened to Seth. Have you been watching the news?"

"No," I replied. "What is it? Was he climbing?"

Did he fall? Was it altitude sickness again?

I'd been preparing myself for this phone call since the first time he left me, eleven years ago.

Heart racing, I waited for Gladys to go on.

"He was on his way to Iceland to be in a movie about that billionaire, George Atherton, but they lost track of the plane. They think they crashed somewhere up north, probably over the Atlantic. I can't believe it."

She began to sob into the phone while I strove to comprehend what I was hearing. I couldn't believe it either. *A plane crash?* Surely there had to be some mistake.

"How many people were on board?" I asked.

"It was just a small private jet so there were only three passengers, plus two pilots. I didn't even know he was going to Iceland. He didn't mention it to me. Did he tell *you?*"

I cupped my forehead in my hand while a wave of nausea crashed over me. "No. The last time we spoke was Christmas Day and he didn't say anything about it. He called from out west, somewhere in the Rockies. Other than that, it's been over a year since we've seen him."

"I'm sorry," she said. "I'm always telling him to go home and be with the two of you, but he never listens. That boy…He was always such a free spirit."

Free spirit…?

How about commitment-phobe?

I exhaled and tried not to think negative thoughts, not at a time like this. "Are they sure the plane actually went down? Is there any chance they just lost contact with it?"

I didn't want to give up hope. Not yet.

"They interviewed Atherton on the news a few minutes ago," Gladys told me. "He's very concerned because the pilots sounded distressed when they last heard from them. They were heading into a storm and wanted to change course, but then they lost contact completely. It was like the plane just disappeared into thin air."

My stomach turned over again. "Oh, God, I can't believe this. Have they started searching yet?"

"Yes, but they don't even know if they're looking in the right place, and now they're saying there are blizzards in the area so they might have to hold off. But if the plane did change course, it could have crashed anywhere. From what I understand, they're searching the waters north of Newfoundland, looking for some sign of the wreckage."

Wreckage. The word turned me into a big puddle of grief. I couldn't bear to think about Seth being on that plane when it was careening from the sky, and how terrifying that must have been.

"This is a nightmare," I said shakily. "What am I going to tell Kaleigh?"

"I don't know," Gladys replied. "But let's not lose hope. I can't accept that he's gone. Not my boy. I have to believe he's still alive out there somewhere."

I nodded and wiped a tear from my eye. "I'll keep my hopes up too, Gladys," I replied, "and I'll say lots of prayers. Keep me posted if you hear anything. And I'll do the same."

We hung up and I took a moment to gather my composure before I went into the living room to tell my daughter that her father's plane had gone missing.

OTHER BOOKS IN THE
COLOR OF HEAVEN SERIES

The COLOR of HEAVEN

A deeply emotional tale about Sophie Duncan, a successful columnist whose world falls apart after her daughter's unexpected illness and her husband's shocking affair. When it seems nothing else could possibly go wrong, her car skids off an icy road and plunges into a frozen lake. There, in the cold dark depths of the water, a profound and extraordinary experience unlocks the surprising secrets from Sophie's past, and teaches her what it means to truly live…and love.

Full of surprising twists and turns and a near-death experience that will leave you breathless, this story is not to be missed.

"A gripping, emotional tale you'll want to read in one sitting."
— *New York Times* bestselling author, Julia London

"Brilliantly poignant mainstream tale."
— 4 ½ starred review, *Romantic Times*

The COLOR of DESTINY

Eighteen years ago a teenage pregnancy changed Kate Worthington's life forever. Faced with many difficult decisions, she chose to follow her heart and embrace an uncertain future with the father of her baby – her devoted first love.

At the same time, in another part of the world, sixteen-year-old Ryan Hamilton makes his own share of mistakes, but learns important lessons along the way. Twenty years later, Kate's and Ryan's paths cross in a way they could never expect, which makes them question the possibility of destiny. Even when all seems hopeless, could it be that everything happens for a reason, and we end up exactly where we are meant to be?

The COLOR *of* HOPE

Diana Moore has led a charmed life. She is the daughter of a wealthy senator and lives a glamorous city life, confident that her handsome live-in boyfriend Rick is about to propose. But everything is turned upside down when she learns of a mysterious woman who works nearby – a woman who is her identical mirror image.

Diana is compelled to discover the truth about this woman's identity, but the truth leads her down a path of secrets, betrayals, and shocking discoveries about her past. These discoveries follow her like a shadow.

Then she meets Dr. Jacob Peterson—a brilliant cardiac surgeon with an uncanny ability to heal those who are broken. With his help, Diana embarks upon a journey to restore her belief in the human spirit, and recover a sense of hope - that happiness, and love, may still be within reach for those willing to believe in second chances.

The COLOR *of*
A DREAM

Nadia Carmichael has had a lifelong run of bad luck. It begins on the day she is born, when she is separated from her identical twin sister and put up for adoption. Twenty-seven years later, not long after she is finally reunited with her twin and is expecting her first child, Nadia falls victim to a mysterious virus and requires a heart transplant.

Now recovering from the surgery with a new heart, Nadia is haunted by a recurring dream that sets her on a path to discover the identity of her donor. Her efforts are thwarted, however, when the father of her baby returns to sue for custody of their child. It's not until Nadia learns of his estranged brother Jesse that she begins to explore the true nature of her dreams, and discover what her new heart truly needs and desires…

The COLOR of A MEMORY

Audrey Fitzgerald believed she was married to the perfect man - a heroic firefighter who saved lives, even beyond his own death. But a year later she meets a mysterious woman who has some unexplained connection to her husband....

Soon Audrey discovers that her husband was keeping secrets and she is compelled to dig into his past. Little does she know... this journey of self-discovery will lead her down a path to a new and different future - a future she never could have imagined.

The COLOR of LOVE

Carla Matthews is a single mother struggling to make ends meet and give her daughter Kaleigh a decent upbringing. When Kaleigh's absent father Seth—a famous alpine climber who never wanted to be tied down—begs for a second chance at fatherhood, Carla is hesitant because she doesn't want to pin her hopes on a man who is always seeking another mountain to scale. A man who was never willing to stay put in one place and raise a family.

But when Seth's plane goes missing after a crash landing in the harsh Canadian wilderness, Carla must wait for news…Is he dead or alive? Will the wreckage ever be found?

One year later, after having given up all hope, Carla receives a phone call that shocks her to her core. A man has been found, half-dead, floating on an iceberg in the North Atlantic, uttering her name. Is this Seth? And is it possible that he will come home to her and Kaleigh at last, and be the man she always dreamed he would be?

The COLOR *of* THE SEASON

Boston cop, Josh Wallace, is having the worst day of his life. First, he's dumped by the woman he was about to propose to, then everything goes downhill from there when he is shot in the line of duty. While recovering in the hospital, he can't seem to forget the woman he wanted to marry, nor can he make sense of the vivid images that flashed before his eyes when he was wounded on the job. Soon, everything he once believed about his life begins to shift when he meets Leah James, an enigmatic resident doctor who somehow holds the key to both his past and his future...

Praise for Julianne MacLean's Historical Romances

꧁ ❦ ꧂

"MacLean's compelling writing turns this simple, classic love story into a richly emotional romance, and by combining engaging characters with a unique, vividly detailed setting, she has created an exceptional tale for readers who hunger for something a bit different in their historical romances."

—BOOKLIST

"You can always count on Julianne MacLean to deliver ravishing romance that will keep you turning pages until the wee hours of the morning."

—Teresa Medeiros

"Julianne MacLean's writing is smart, thrilling, and sizzles with sensuality."

—Elizabeth Hoyt

"Scottish romance at its finest, with characters to cheer for, a lush love story, and rousing adventure. I was captivated from the very first page. When it comes to exciting Highland romance, Julianne MacLean delivers."

—Laura Lee Guhrke

"She is just an all-around wonderful writer, and I look forward to reading everything she writes."

—*Romance Junkies*

About the Author

Julianne MacLean is a USA Today bestselling author of many historical romances, including The Highlander Series with St. Martin's Press and her popular American Heiress Series with Avon/Harper Collins. She also writes contemporary mainstream fiction, and The Color of Heaven was a USA Today bestseller. She is a three-time RITA finalist, and has won numerous awards, including the Booksellers' Best Award, the Book Buyer's Best Award, and a Reviewers' Choice Award from Romantic Times for Best Regency Historical of 2005. She lives in Nova Scotia with her husband and daughter, and is a dedicated member of Romance Writers of Atlantic Canada. Please visit Julianne's website for more information and to subscribe to her mailing list to stay informed about upcoming releases.

OTHER BOOKS BY
JULIANNE MACLEAN

The American Heiress Series:
To Marry the Duke
An Affair Most Wicked
My Own Private Hero
Love According to Lily
Portrait of a Lover
Surrender to a Scoundrel

The Pembroke Palace Series:
In My Wildest Fantasies
The Mistress Diaries
When a Stranger Loves Me
Married By Midnight
A Kiss Before the Wedding - A Pembroke Palace Short Story
Seduced at Sunset

The Highlander Series:
Captured by the Highlander
Claimed by the Highlander
Seduced by the Highlander
The Rebel – A Highland Short Story

The Royal Trilogy:
Be My Prince
Princess in Love
The Prince's Bride

Harlequin Historical Romances:
Prairie Bride
The Marshal and Mrs. O'Malley
Adam's Promise

Time Travel Romance
Taken by the Cowboy

Contemporary Fiction:
The Color of Heaven
The Color of Destiny
The Color of Hope
The Color of a Dream
The Color of a Memory
The Color of Love
The Color of the Season
The Color of Joy

CPSIA information can be obtained
at www.ICGtesting.com
Printed in the USA
LVOW11s2252181017
552959LV00001B/114/P